LET'S SMILE AGAIN

RE-VISITING FAMILY LIFE IN THE SEVENTIES

by

JEAN HILL

Let's Smile Again

Is dedicated to the memory of my Mum and Dad

Constance and Robert Marchant

And to my Aunt and Uncle

Elsie and Dick Butchers

(They feature as 'elderly relatives')

Take a rambling meander re-visiting
Family Life in the Seventies

Elderly relatives assembling a flat-pack

Other work by Jean Hill

"The Sting In The Tale"

and

"The Barb In The Rhyme"

**Poems and Short Stories
to make you laugh and cry**

**Available from: Lulu.com
or
Amazon**

TURN BACK THE PAGES

Dictated by the pattern of life, generations are lost to us, and those to whom I have dedicated this book were much loved, are greatly missed, and no longer with us. I now take their place in the generation game.

When Auntie Elsie, my mother's twin, died I had the sad task of sorting through her paper-work. Whilst doing so I came across all the published magazine and newspaper cuttings of articles that I had written in the 70's, carefully preserved in a plastic bag.

As a tribute to generations past, I have re-produced these articles. Although, of course, dated as per the era, they reflect family life in the 70's and funny moments from all those years ago.

I hope you will find 'Let's Smile Again' interesting and amusing reading.

ACKNOWLEDGEMENTS

Deborah and **Samantha**
for being so hugely supportive
in the practical production of this book.
Without your skill and patience it would
never have happened.

Sharon ... for continued encouragement.

Robin ... for the front cover photography.

Benjamin and **Jamie** ... for just being.

THANK-YOU ALL

PARENTING PITFALLS

As parents do you ever wonder if you'll manage to rear your children to reach adulthood? I do, and frighten myself to death! As a parent I'm a total failure!

From the time we walked up the aisle in the early 60's I've wanted a baby and now, seven years later, baby is on its way. I'm over the moon; husband is shell-shocked – I don't think he's worked out how it happened yet. But the hospital soon prick my euphoric balloon – they class me as an 'older mother'. I suppose a first baby at the ripe old age of twenty-five is pushing it a bit ... but even so! At least I qualify for free orange juice.

And now ... this very afternoon, I'm bringing home our gorgeous six-day old baby girl and I'm scared witless. Husband tries to help but I know men don't really have a clue what it's all about. "I've ordered an extra pint of milk from the milkman" he says. "What for?" is my puzzled response. "Well, that's what babies drink, isn't it?" I can see this is going to be an uphill struggle.

We set ourselves up – new parents on a mission. The Milton Set to sterilize bottles sits on top of the 'fridge along with the budgie's cage and the yellow Napisan bucket lurks pulsating under the sink. And, we're off! But how can one little new-born occupy the time of two adults 24/7? Anyway, exhausted or not, the nappies need washing and, in anticipation of this demanding new arrival, we've bought a washing machine. There it stands, a Hoover Keymatic with a sloping front, just waiting to do the first wash. I know all about washing machines having spent every Friday night in the launderette from the day we were married. In fact, we heard that President Kennedy had been shot while we were watching the washing go round – Friday, 22nd November, 1963 – a few years ago now.

Having carefully removed the worst of the soil collected in the muslin liners, the nappies soaked overnight in Napisan, I put in the first load for its opening performance. The new Terry Towelling nappies went into the machine a gleaming pristine white – I've seen the Persil advert and want to be a 'Mum That Knows' – but extricating the tangled mass a couple of hours later I'm stunned to find they've all turned a yellow-grey colour – shock-horror! Realisation dawns – I'd picked up a yellow duster with the load and the colour has stained all the nappies! I shed a disproportionate number of tears over this. I'm told that's due to an affliction called 'baby-blues' and I just have to get over and get on with it. I seem to spend my life walking round in my dressing-gown crying these days! Oh well, nobody cares so I better had get on with it. The ruined nappies will still do the job intended and they can be hidden under the rubber pants with the pink frill. But how I cope with the shame when I hang them on the line to dry is another matter. I'll definitely be known as 'The Mum That Doesn't Know!'

Being new parents isn't easy. Husband takes himself off to work each morning bleary-eyed having spent the entire night trying to pacify a screaming child with colic. The proportion of gripe-water to milk has reached the 50/50 mark – she's probably hooked on it.

To get out of the house I put her in her brand new, state of the art, no expense spared (her Granny bought it for us!)

pram. The body of the pram lifts off the wheels and I can lay it on the back seat of the car – brilliant. Anyway, we walk to the library – and she's stopped screaming. I leave her in the library entrance sleeping peacefully while I choose two or three books. It's a nice day, and needing a couple of stamps, off I go, across the road, and walk a few hundred yards to the post office. Standing in the queue I go cold. Where's the baby? I can't even think straight for a minute or two. Then, remembering, I break out of the queue, in which I've been standing for at least ten minutes, and run like a mad woman back to the library. And there she is, still sleeping soundly. Me? – I'm sobbing with relief and have to sit down. The responsibility is overwhelming and this is just the beginning.

Somehow our baby daughter survives and three and a half years later she's about to have a brother or a sister. There's no way of knowing which, but as long as it's healthy I don't mind.

Daughter Number Two arrives. Apart from her deciding to start to be born on the level crossing instead of waiting until we get to the hospital, all goes well. I was too late to have any pethidine and I was really looking forward to that! The nurse asks husband if he wants to stay for the birth. Apparently they can nowadays. I've never seen him move so quickly in his life – out the door! Just as well I suppose; the hospital have enough to cope with without all that shrieking, fainting and throwing-up (he can't even cut up meat!). And I might make the odd grunt or two as well!

Anyway, we're experienced parents now and first outing with Daughter Number Two is to take her on a shopping trip in the next town which involves negotiating a steep flight of concrete steps to an underpass. Husband hauls out the body of the pram in which she is sleeping and places it on the wheels and off we go. All is well until we reach the steps of the underpass and try to go down them by tilting the pram which husband is pushing. Unfortunately he has forgotten that the pram body has to be **clipped** to the wheels to secure it in position and it careers out of control down the steps, leaving him holding the handle to the pram wheels! As it bowls past me a few paces in front, I pluck our precious four-day old daughter out by the scruff of her little yellow jacket and she is dangled mid-air as the pram body tumbles over and over, bouncing down the steps. Have you ever seen a man with a face the colour of someone who has died a thousand deaths in less than ten seconds? Somehow Daughter Number Two survives!

How quickly they grow and, in spite of us, flourish. Daughter Number One is very good at tantrums – especially in shoe shops. At three years old she wants totally unsuitable red shoes with buckles and bows – and it's mid-winter. I decide to teach her a lesson by walking out of the shoe shop and leave her behind yelling and screaming and flinging herself all over the floor. I actually wait just outside the door in the green-grocer's queue thinking she will tire of the tantrum and follow me. Does she heck! Next thing I hear is the shoe shop manager yelling and screaming at me as well. I vow she'll go bare foot before I try to buy her another pair of shoes.

Daughter Number Two is not prone to tantrums but she has inherited what the family call 'The Look'. She can kill at a hundred paces. Here we are, some years later, standing in the same green-grocer's queue (they know me quite well there now) and she starts. "Mum, Mum, is that a witch?" I try to shush her. "Mum, Mum, it is a witch, look it is (foot stamp). *It is a witch*", louder and louder. She peers round the 'witch', probably looking for a broom-stick, to prove her point. At this stage, the sweet-faced nun turns round to confront us. "See, I said it's a witch" says child, giving her 'the look'. I'm still stuttering my embarrassed apologies while the green-grocer is weighing out my pound of sprouts!

But, resilient as ever, they grow up. Eldest daughter plays the piano really well – we listen to 'The Entertainer' until our ears ache. And, in my biased opinion, she's good at ballet dancing too. It's just her ballet teacher doesn't recognise talent when she sees it right in front of her pirouetting, arabesque(ing) and par de deux(ing)! The silly woman's just written an end-of-term report saying 'She dances like a footballer'. Oh, the shame. That's the last tutu I'm buying!

But it's youngest daughter who is using 'the look' to great effect. She hates piano lessons and, apart from thumping out 'chopsticks' just to annoy me, won't practise her scales. And now she's deliberately dropped her music book down the back of the piano, and her lesson is due in ten minutes time! The music teacher ends up having a nervous breakdown. I'm not surprised really. I've teetered on the edge of a nervous breakdown ever since they were born.

But it's all worth it. When youngest daughter is picked to play 'Mary' in the nursery school nativity, and when eldest is chosen to narrate her junior school play, your heart nearly bursts with love and pride and you recognise how barren life would have been without them. I hope I survive to see them have children of their own – then they'll know what it's all about!

THAT SINKING FEELING

"Shall we go on holiday?" "What", I gurgle. Why do husbands always ask these questions at such stupid moments? Here I am, a couple of months into my second pregnancy, with my head down the loo, re-visiting my breakfast, and he wants to know if we should go on holiday.

What with heaving my heart up every hour or so, not to mention coping with the trauma that only a two-year old toddler with temper tantrums can inflict, perhaps it isn't the most appropriate time to ask.

"We could go to Butlin's and stay in one of their chalets". Oh, joy, whoopee, a week spent self-catering in a garden shed. Everybody else seems to be going to the Costa Something in Spain. Still, I suppose 'chalet' sounds a bit more posh when we tell our friends where we're going.

And so, here we are, a few months later, packing husband's brand spanking new Mini Clubman, which is the centre of his whole existence, and to me resembles a brown box on wheels. But, hey, what do I know about cars? I know I don't like brown!

Does my opinion count with 'him indoors' – NO! In the pecking order, two-year old toddler comes first, second and third. He idolizes our little daughter (well, don't all Dads?) and she already knows how to twist him completely round her little finger with inbred feminine wiles, pretty smiles and tear filled eyes when she doesn't get her own way.

Thinking about it, next, in order of priority, comes 'The Car' with more attention lavished on it than I ever get, followed closely by the dog, who flirts with him with wagging tail, big brown eyes and licky kisses – I could learn a lot from our dog – though I draw the line at licky kisses!

He likes the hamster too; a sort of love-hate relationship there since the vicious little brute bit right through his finger when he was hand-feeding it sunflower seeds. You've never seen such a performance, blood dripping off his elbow as he leapt around the room.

Me? I rate alongside the stick-insects; but, come to think of it, I actually skivvy for them, cleaning out the goldfish bowl in which they live and raiding the neighbour's hedge for privet to feed them.

Oh well, that's me, a skivvy to two stick-insects. Perhaps I should stand up and shout the odds sometimes or burn my bra. That seems popular at the moment. I could dig out the one with loose elastic and set fire to it. I would if I thought anyone would care or even notice. But if I ever muster up the energy to join Women's Lib they'll all know about it. Solidarity sisters – God, I'm exhausted just thinking about it. Oh well, where's the duster? – The stick-insects are looking at me again.

Anyway, I was telling you about our 1971 holiday at Butlin's. We now have everything we need for a week's self-catering holiday with a toddler who only eats chocolate, fish fingers and the yolks of boiled eggs. Finally we're off.

Let me ask you – how do you get your husband to stop on a journey? Here we are, bowling along, hour after hour without a break, when two-year old toddler decides she wants to wee. Not at the next service station or convenient stopping place, but NOW! In desperation I put the little pink potty we carry around with us in the space between the driver and passenger seats and sit her on it.

While said child is duly performing, husband's only concern is that nothing is slopped or splashed in his new car. So intent is he on what's going on between the seats that he fails to notice the car in front has stopped and runs slap, bang, wallop, straight into the back of it. Child, pink potty, and gallons of wee fly in all directions. Not the best start to our week. We can work out what to put on the insurance claim later.

So we arrive, the squarish brown box on wheels (sorry, Mini Clubman) with a bashed in front, reeking of wee and vomit, and husband crying silently as only men can do to extract the utmost sympathy when they think they're hard done by. And here they are, our very own row of pre-fabricated garden-sheds. To be fair, it's not too bad. It's clean(ish) and has a fridge which is a plus. The grey carpet (not sure what colour it was originally) has some pretty suspicious stains on it. The sun's come out and with the determination of the typical British family holiday maker – we're going to enjoy ourselves.

All in all, the weather is kind and we do have a nice time. Toddler buries Dad in the sand and we spend a painful half-hour digging grit out of his eyes. I stop being sick and toddler over-comes her fear of falling off pink potties.

But the highlight of our holiday – the one incident that gives us the biggest laugh and will provide the funniest memory, is thanks to the 'Family Fat'. Mother Fat, Father Fat and Teenage Son Fat. And when I say 'Fat', I mean FAT with a capital 'F'.

Butlin's has an over-head mono-rail. We spend hours on it as it is cheaper than taking our little daughter on fair-ground rides. So, here we are, high up on the mono-rail, with a lovely, friendly driver in the front section, smoothly traversing the holiday camp with the boating lake underneath us. And down below, getting into a very small rowing boat, is the Family Fat; Mother Fat, in a flowery frock sitting one end of the boat, Father Fat, with handkerchief tied in four corners on his head to protect him from the sun, sitting at the other end, and their lardy son in the middle. The boating lake attendant shoves them off from the edge and teenage son clamps his podgy hands around the oars and starts to row.

With the boat getting lower and lower in the water, they make about twenty yards out into the centre before it ever so slowly starts to sink. The drama that follows equals that of the Titanic. Mother Fat starts screaming, Father Fat tries to stand up and Teenage Fat continues to splash the oars up and down.

I suppose the water in the lake is only about four feet deep but the over-loaded boat and its three occupants, still gripping the sides, sink below the water. With much screaming and yelling and thrashing of arms they finally stand up in the stricken vessel and the boating lake attendant wades out chest-deep to extricate them from the boat.

Father Fat, with knotted handkerchief miraculously still knotted on his head, Mother Fat, with flowery dress floating midriff and exhibiting pink drawers elasticated just above the knee, along with Teenage Fat, puce coloured acne wetly glistening on his pasty face in the reflection of the lake, are assisted ashore.

On the mono-rail, which has stopped because the driver is laughing too much to drive, we have a ring-side balcony seat. I'm surprised the train stays on the rails as it is shaking with all our laughter. Daughter, just approaching three, is convulsed. I only hope she is not too young to remember the incident.

I can hear you saying – "You should be ashamed of yourself for laughing at other folk's misfortune". And, yes, I am ashamed. Once I've stopped laughing I really will be – honestly!

This holiday's turned out quite well, all things considered!

FOREIGN EXCHANGE

All families undergo tough times and 1972 is a difficult year. With a baby, and a three year old toddler, going out to work to help with the family finances is a non-starter – who would look after them?

Husband works all the hours God sends and is never home much before seven in the evening; so what's left for me to do? Bar-work – I tried that! Being ogled by a lot of old men propping up the bar is a dignity-stripper. At least my tough old East Acton Secondary Modern School taught me how to deal with the unwanted attention of men when they've had a few. I've a razor-sharp tongue and, if there's one thing I'm good at, it's quick response and sarky repartee, and I can put down any amorous block-head before his chat-up lines have left his mouth, followed by a look that kills at a hundred paces. And if another nerd pats my bottom when I'm out there collecting glasses, he's going to end up wearing his pint instead of drinking it! No, I'm not cut out for bar-work.

Unqualified night nursing at a local hospital – well – I stick that for three years in a state of permanent exhaustion. All day looking after a toddler, up all night emptying bed-pans and laying out the dead, followed by up again all the next day caring for our child, reduces me to a zombie state. But the money's good – £8 for a twelve hour night shift.

So now – my new venture. 'Let's take in foreign exchange students'. Brilliant idea – Oh Yeah! Our house is inspected and me, baby, toddler and cat are all on our best behaviour. I almost wring my hands with grovelling servitude, hoping to pass the test. I've even dusted the skirting boards and

17

Hoovered under the beds. We've a nice spare bedroom, two single beds and, to make it worthwhile, I want two students. Apparently they have to be the same sex (I'll go along with that – don't want any shenanigans in our spare room), but they have to be of different nationality so that they can only communicate with each other and us in English.

First to arrive is Gerta from Germany. Husband has to go to Victoria to meet her off the train. Don't men get arrested trying to pick up foreign girls at railway stations? Anyway, they meet up, more by luck than judgement, and he brings her home. She's not impressed by the fact that we don't have a shower so, waiting for the immersion to heat some water for a bath (it's not on because this is not our bath night), I offer an egg on toast for her tea. She's not impressed with that either. This is going to be more difficult than I thought.

Next to arrive is Sophie from France and they hate each other on sight. She doesn't like tea to drink and wants coffee. Ah – success! I know foreigners drink coffee and I've got a jar of Maxwell House – see – no expense spared. But that's wrong too – she wants frothy-coffee. How the hell do I make that? Perhaps I should add a few Lux Soap Flakes! Frothy-coffee – what next, I ask you?

Our diet revolves around baked beans and chips so this is going to be an uphill struggle. As a treat I put squares of cheese and pineapple chunks on cocktail sticks (I've never had a cocktail, but the sticks come in handy), and I poke them in a potato to look like a hedgehog. I do this to impress elderly relatives but it leaves the foreign exchange students cold! I try to talk 'food' to Sophie as, by now, both the

18

students are on the point of starvation and I'm tearing my hair out wondering what to feed them on.

Sophie says she likes *escargot*. (That's snails to you and me). We have a few snails lurking under our rhubarb, but the thought of them looking at me from the middle of a puddle of baked beans doesn't appeal. She also says she likes *grenouille* (frogs' legs)! What do French cooks do with the rest of the frog? I have hysterical visions of millions of frogs hopping around France on wooden legs!

Both Gerta and Sophie inform me that they like chicken. Well – they can go on liking chicken – we can only afford chicken for a treat. We have one at Christmas. What's the matter with the really nice dinner of neck-of-lamb stew we had last night. I put two Oxo cubes in that! And that tasty bit of brisket with roast potatoes done in dripping we had at the weekend? I suppose they're only used to rump-steak. Mind you, I like a tender piece of rump. I always choose that if, on rare occasions, we go to a Berni Inn, for my birthday.

My Granny always said 'You can't go wrong with a joint of beef at the weekend'. I've remembered that. She was right. Left-over cold beef is lovely on a Monday when you're too busy to cook and have all the washing to do. (At least I have a washing machine now and don't have to sit in the launderette). And, with a bit of luck, there's enough left over for mince on Tuesday.

But the best part of having beef is the lovely pot of dripping with the meat juice turning to jelly at the bottom. We have that on toast for our tea – hot toast and beef dripping loaded with lumps of meat jelly – wonderful with plenty of salt sprinkled on top! 'That'll put hairs on your chest' as my Granny used to say. I spent most of my childhood eating lumps of dripping and having camphorated oil rubbed into my chest!

Gerta says she would like *bratwurst*. I think that's some sort of German sausage. I try to comply by putting haslet in her sandwiches – that's made from minced pork offal I think, but she doesn't seem to like that either. Anyway, tonight it's tripe and onions followed by tapioca pudding. Good stuff. They should think themselves lucky. I was brought up on spam and cabbage and, if I'd been good, a sugar and condensed milk sandwich!

I'm losing the will to live here. Toddler only eats egg yolks, fish-fingers and chocolate, supplemented by spoonfuls of Malt which she actually quite likes! Baby lives on Farley's Rusks and milk – that's easy – and Gerta and Sophie continue to starve. Perhaps we'll have better luck with the next two students. Husband exists on a concoction of whatever's left over by the time he arrives home from work! Me – I console myself with Mars Bars. I eat lots of Mars Bars!

With relief we wave 'good-bye' to Gerta and Sophie and welcome Riza from Austria and Dominque from France. First argument, after being in the house for a whole two minutes, is with Riza who, at fifteen, wants to smoke in my living room. I hate smoking and firmly tell her it's not allowed. She spends most of the next two weeks smoking at the bottom of our garden. Well, that's not altogether correct, how could I forget the night she set fire to the bed by smoking underneath the blankets!

Dominque is another kettle of fish. She's the spoilt brat of an aristocratic French family. Only last year we had the telephone installed in our house and now she's racking up a colossal bill by making long distance calls to France. We'll need another mortgage to pay for her chats and complaints about us, delivered in rapid French resembling machine gun fire, with Mama and Papa in some chateau in the Dordogne. I'm really sorry that she's home-sick – I think they have a maid at home to pander to her each and every whim. So, with Dominque crying up in her room and Riza at the bottom of the garden, at least they're less trouble than the first two.

The season is coming to an end – can we survive two more? Along come Chantal and Marcia – both from France. I think the organizers have forgotten that they should be of different nationality if they come to our house or else they're getting desperate. Chantal and Marcia only speak to each other – they ignore us completely!

Actually, I quite like Marcia from Marseilles – butter wouldn't melt, etc. – that is until she is caught shop-lifting in Woolworths. I banish her to her room and tell her that husband will speak to her parents later – I've got a splitting headache with the stress she's caused so husband can deal with this one. He'll go mad when he comes in from work – just what he needs at the end of a long working day! Meanwhile I have to talk to the student exchange organizers and lock up our valuables! Laying out the dead and emptying bed-pans all night seems a doddle compared with hosting exchange students!

But, all in all, Chantal proves to be the biggest headache. She fancies husband! Now some husbands might be flattered by the attention of a sixteen year-old French Lolita called Chantal – he is terrified! Each night she changes into a skimpy negligée and drapes herself around the kitchen doorway to catch him unawares as he arrives home at six forty-five. She is shameless. I think it's funny to see the look on his face – he shields himself by holding his briefcase in front of him while edging his way through the door. I usually come to his rescue by telling her to get dressed properly or stay in her room. Oh God – will the summer of '72 never end!

And now, many years on, youngest daughter is approaching her teenage years. She presents me with a letter from school: 'Dear Parent – Would you like your daughter to be part of a student exchange scheme? There is a family in Marseilles ready to welcome her'. Marseilles – I remember Marcia.

If there's one thing I've instilled into both daughters, it's to be honest. If you can't afford it – you can't have it. I know they've moaned a bit – they were the last children in their class to have a colour television – if I listen to them, we're the last family to have everything. I think I've got the point across – even though they give me pitying looks when I say that we appreciate things more if we have to wait and save up for them. As with most families, life gets a little easier as the years pass. I work now the children are older so we can afford for her to go on an exchange trip.

Dear God, if I let her go to Marseilles, please don't let them teach her to be a shop-lifter!

HOPPING MAD

Hopping mad – yes, I really am. Some rotten blighter has just pinched the hub caps off my little Allegro. Nice shiny ones they were too; not exactly polished by me, but husband – who has a feeling for cars and doesn't see them as metal boxes for transporting people from place to place as I do – was often to be seen with a can of chrome cleaner in his hand buffing up the hub-caps.

And what's really getting up my nose is the fact that millions of pounds are being spent on refurbishing our prisons, equipping them with gymnasiums, educational facilities, TV's etc. and then we find out that's there's not enough money left in the kitty to pay the police to catch the little thugs so that they can enjoy the benefit of all these wonderful amenities. I don't suppose there's any danger of someone waking up to the fact that basic accommodation (and a diet of bread and water for those who pinch hub-caps) might be less attractive to the criminals and leave a little money over to pay the police.

I've just had somebody knock the door to ask if I want to contribute money for the welfare of prisoners' wives. Yeah, yeah, can you see that little pink pig flying past! On your bike, matey! I've got four new hub-caps to buy.

FROM NIGHTMARE TO REALITY

There is nothing odd or unusual about me. An ordinary house-wife living in an ordinary house, with the regulation number of children. But a few years ago something happened to me in the early hours of a summer morning which was anything but ordinary. To this day, thinking about the strange experience of that morning makes the hairs on my arms stand to attention. A prickly sensation creeps all over me.

It all started when we were given an old fish tank. Not knowing very much about keeping tropical fish, and with the aid of a library book, we set about buying all the bits of equipment we needed to keep the water aerated and at the right temperature We collected dozens of shells, bought gravel, plants and rocks; and finally stocked the four-foot wide tank with fish. We quickly learned some lessons: that angel fish eat guppies, and that direct sunlight makes algae grow.

Then we bought the blue fish.

It was just an ordinary fish. About an inch and a half long, and bluish in colour. It made quite an attractive addition to the tank.

Then a strange thing happened. After a week or so the blue fish just disappeared. I wasn't deeply distressed, but I'll admit that I was uneasy. How could it have vanished? It was too big to have been attacked by other fish. After a couple of days of peering into the tank, we reached the conclusion that it must have died and been eaten by the tank's other inhabitants.

And this is where the story stops being ordinary and the macabre takes over. I am only grateful that what you are about to read was witnessed by my husband, otherwise surely my own sanity would be seriously in question and my experience would be heard with obvious disbelief.

The night was warm, and we had few covers on the bed. My sleep was restful and untroubled. Then I was possessed by a dream; a dream which became a nightmare.

I was swimming around peacefully. Other fish darted past me and I was aware of light shimmering on my silver-blue scales. The water sparkled. Ahead of me was an opening, waiting to be explored. It looked cool and inviting. I approached it, a little hesitantly at first; but something was drawing me towards it.

Inside, it was darker, but still I went on, around a narrow, pearly, spiral bend until I could go no further. I tried to turn around and head back to the peaceful waters outside but I found I couldn't. I struggled to turn in the confined space, but my body only became wedged tighter and tighter between the smooth, cool walls. The water was pounding in my head as I thrashed wildly to free myself, writhing and twisting fruitlessly. Pain seared my broken and exhausted body. I knew I was very near death, and a terrifying panic engulfed me.

I shot up in bed, my body wet with perspiration and shaking uncontrollably, the sound of rushing water still in my ears.

My husband was suddenly shaken out of his sleep when I shouted, "I know where the fish is, I know where the fish is". I jumped out of bed and, without stopping for a dressing gown, I ran down the stairs, dragging him along with me. Crying hysterically, I pointed wildly at one of the shells we had put on the bottom of the tank. "I'm … it's … in there. I've been in there. I'm sure. I know."

Rolling up his pyjama sleeve, my husband put his arm into the tank. There were many shells, all of a similar type, but I knew, without a doubt, which one it was. With my finger stabbing at the glass, he located the one shell among the many which tastefully decorated the tank, and plucked it from the water. "It's just an empty shell", he said. "For heaven's sake, calm down".

But I knew beyond any doubt that the blue fish was inside. Steadying myself, I asked my husband to bring a hammer. He laid the wet shell on some old newspaper on the kitchen floor, and tapped it, gently at first, and then with a bit more force. The shell cracked open. There was the pearly bend that I had swum past, and the familiar smooth walls of the inner shell. And there, also, its body still glistening, was the blue fish, in exactly the position I had known it would be.

My husband sat back on his heels, his face as white as mine. All he could say over and over again was "How did you know? How did you know?"

Did I somehow tune in to the death throes of the blue fish as it struggled and thrashed inside the shell? Was there some form of telepathic communication? Whatever the answer, the trauma I experienced can never be exorcised. It will haunt me for ever.

The incident was so unnerving that we gave the tank and its contents away. Never again shall I risk the living death of the blue fish.

(Unbelievable but true)

LET LOVE ENCIRCLE ALL

We're NOT having a dog and that's final! I see the secret smile of conspiracy pass between Daughter Number One (aged 7) and Daughter Number Two (aged 4). Youngest daughter, helped by her sister, actually writes a little note which starts ... 'Please, Daddy' ... and ends with lots of kisses.

Ginge, our ginger tom, who has been Top Cat of the house for the past ten years, sidles up to husband to present a united front on the question of a dog entering the family. I sit back and watch events unfold. Coming from a doggy family, I'd quite like a dog, but my intervention is superfluous. All the male bonding in the world between cat and husband will never match the feminine wiles employed by two blonde daughters with big brown eyes and unshed crocodile tears quivering on lashes. He's doomed!

"The cat's quite enough trouble as it is", he goes on, ignoring Ginge's indignant, hard-done-by, glare. Well, he's right there I suppose. Ginge has taken up fishing in next door's pond and I spend half my life resuscitating gold-fish and sneaking them back over the fence under the cover of darkness.

Ginge

But, anyway, here we are, one month on, with a little bundle of chestnut curls and big brown eyes (sound familiar?) sitting in the palm of my hand. And husband is captivated – well, he will be when he stops moaning about how much she cost.

Wendy

I recognise immediately that I've gone down a peg or two in the pecking order. Daughters come joint first, now followed by the dog (it's the eyes!), the cat and the car following closely. I cling to the bottom rung of the ladder because I guess I'm quite useful. I cook, wash, shop and clean for all of them. Hey-ho, that's my role in life.

He's such a 'softie', my husband. No wonder I love him to bits. Look at the time we had an invasion of mice in our French farmhouse. We take ourselves off to the local *quincaillerie* and spend umpteen francs on a humane trap, catching one mouse each night, and then releasing it half a mile away next morning. Problem is, we can only catch one at a time and we don't want to be trailing along the lane through the woods to release it at three o'clock in the morning. So, it has to stay inside the humane trap, making a noise and enjoying the slab of cheddar I put in there, until the next day.

So, husband has this bright idea. We put a smooth-sided plastic dustbin outside on the slope that comes up level with our bedroom window and put each mouse we catch during the night into it. Then we take them en masse up the lane in the morning. This works well; we catch five individual little mice (we don't get much sleep) and they are duly put through the open bedroom window into the nice clean dustbin below.

Finally – sleep! At seven we wake to the sound of pounding rain. "That's some thunder-storm out there" says me. "Oh My God! The Mice!" Husband, clad only in his pyjamas and socks, leaps out of bed, races round the L-shaped farmhouse to our back bedroom window in rain coming down in stair-rods, a howling gale, deafened by thunder-claps and dodging lightning strikes, to find five little mice doing the breast-stroke. They are all hurriedly tipped out and, having been rescued, scuttle under the hedge and live to tell the tale. Husband? – Oh – he resembles one drowned rat!

The French Farmhouse

And, it's not just the mice at the farmhouse – we worry about the lizards too. The house was built circa 1650 and needs quite a lot of maintenance. This time we're rendering the external walls of the pig-pens. Having brought a cement mixer across the channel – that caused a bit of a problem at customs I can tell you – we're now busy slapping cement all over the exposed brick-work. Problem is, lizards live in the walls – including tiny baby ones. How could we be so heartless and cement up their front-doors. So – obviously, we leave little openings every few inches so that they can continue occupancy of our pig-pen walls. Our French friends worry about us sometimes.

But, back to the newest addition to our family – a gorgeous brown poodle called Wendy. The cat treats her with total disdain but she has husband in the palm of her four little paws. First night, which dictates the pattern for the rest of her life, husband says "You can't leave her in the kitchen – she's crying!" He always leaps to attention at the first murmuring, attention seeking, sounds of distress from the daughters – and he's just as bad with the dog. So, here she is, snuggled in between us, and here she stays! Every evening he comes in from work and opens the back door saying "How's my little love, then? Who's Daddy's beautiful girl?" She answers with her tail and her eyes – she says 'Where's the choccy-drops and it's time for walkies'. All I get from him is "What's for dinner?" Our dog could give me a few lessons on how to get round a man!

But, fourteen years on, as we all know it will happen, is the day of great sadness. Wendy has gone to the great doggy-heaven in the sky and we are all heart-broken. I've never seen my six-foot-two chunky husband cry before but tears stream down his face as he digs a small grave in the garden and I wrap her little brown curled body in her favourite crocheted blanket and we place her in it and say 'Goodbye'. This is going to take some getting over.

Sadly Ginge died a few years ago and now daughters have their Dad cornered again. "No, we're NOT having another cat and that's final". Oh Yeah! And so arrives Oliver, another ginger tom.

Oliver is the luckiest cat that ever lived. If nine lives is the cat average, he must have ninety-nine. We don't intentionally mean to have Oliver – he is sort of thrust upon us, and Dad gives in, as I know he will, under daughter pressure.

A farm near where my sister lives is inundated with wild cats – feral I guess. Anyway, the whole cat community is struck down with cat 'flu. This is a killer and causes great suffering to the animals. The farmer, a very humane man, calls in the RSPCA to put down the entire cat population to relieve their misery. This is duly done. Once the RSPCA have left, out from the bottom of a drain pipe, where he has been hiding, pops this tiny shivering five-week old kitten. Yes, you've guessed – Oliver. He is a pitiful sight. He is temporarily blinded by a membrane covering his eyes caused by this foul disease, his little face covered with mucus from his ears, mouth and eyes, just a fragile scrap of bones and matted ginger fur.

Well, what can you do? Yes, daft as we are, we wrap him up and bring him home. Although he comes from wild and feral parentage, he is too ill and weak to care and allows us to tend him. He instantly adopts us as 'his family'.

Next morning our troubles start with a visit to the vet. "You've got a very sick diseased kitten" the vet says, his tone disparaging and condemning. "You should always choose a healthy kitten from a healthy litter". Faced with my resolute and determined po-faced expression, I banish any thoughts he may be having about lethal injections! "OK, well, I'll see what I can do but don't hold out much hope", he says.

So, with injections, pills, ear-drops, eye-drops and copious tender loving care (not to mention an astronomical vet's bill), we begin our crusade to save Oliver. We feed him every few hours with a syringe, I rush home from work each lunch-time (a round sixteen mile trip) to administer medication, daughters take up nursing care on their return from school, and husband undertakes night-duty. And Oliver thrives.

Oliver

Six weeks later and the vet is reversing his previous somewhat caustic comments. "Nice healthy little cat you have here" he says. I refer him to his previous notes and he takes another look. Even vets have egg on their faces sometimes!

Oliver is the most loving and affectionate animal you could wish for. Here he lays, cradled in my arms, on his back with paws in the air, purring his head off, while I play *'Round and Round the Garden, Like a Teddy-Bear, One Step, Two Steps and Tickle You Under There'* on his tummy. I know – daft as a brush – who me or the cat?

But, breeding will out, and Oliver is an absolute menace to everybody else and we have to warn people not to touch him – he draws blood on anyone putting out a hand in his direction. But we are his family and the bond of mutual love is obvious and unbreakable. He never leaves our side.

We are so lucky to have had Ginge, Wendy and Oliver as part of our lives. Teaching children, by example, to love, respect, care and show compassion for animals is a vital part of a child's up-bringing. Although my parenting skills fall far short of perfect, at least I hope I've done that.

Without the bark of a dog, the purr of a cat, and the laughter of children, our home would have been a very barren place.

BLESS THEM ALL

If anyone ever asks my religion I always say "Agnostic" – don't know what it means but in a National Opinion Poll I think I'd be in with the 'Don't Knows'. However, being a hypocrite as well as a heathen, I drag my protesting children into church on every possible occasion. So, when eldest daughter was asked by the Guides to do a reading one Sunday, I feigned great delight and every encouragement was given.

I had a couple of elderly relatives, poor souls, staying with me that week, so rehearsals of the reading, held in competition with the telly in our sitting room, were well supported with us all genuflecting and saying Amen in the right places.

Eldest daughter, very worried that when the big day came the congregation wouldn't know when to make the right responses, persuaded us along with her for moral support (with the exception of Dad who went off to fly his model 'plane!). I'm not sure what I was supposed to do – perhaps prod a few members who looked in danger of nodding off, or open a soup kitchen to revive those overcome by the cold.

Anyway, apart from pronouncing the name of the Devil as 'Saturn', the reading was audible and responses loud and clear – I rubbed my sweaty palms on the inside of my gloves and thought that my troubles were over. I need not have rung the doctor for those extra Valium after all!

Oh, how wrong can you be, poor deluded fool that I am. To take elderly relatives to church is asking for trouble with a capital 'T'. I should have backed out when Elderly Relative

Number Two asked: "Is this a 'Pedestrian' Church?" I haven't a clue where the nearest Presbyterian Church is and, as he is a Baptist anyway, I didn't think it mattered. Storm clouds gathered with the incense. Loud muttering about not liking high church drowned my reverent prayers asking God to render him silent for the remainder of the service.

In my other ear, Elderly Relative Number One was audibly enquiring where the non-existent toilet was, and "Does this go on for much longer?"

Big trouble came when the congregation arose to take Holy Communion. "Where are they going?" asked youngest child. "To take bread and wine, dear" I answered. "I don't want any" was the reply. Feeling this was best under the circumstances I suggested we all sit and freeze in silence for the next few minutes.

That was when elderly relative informs small child that at the other end of the queue the vicar is serving chocolate eclairs and Pepsi-Cola. I hate uncontrollable children who shriek "I want some" during Holy Communion. A kind friend came to the rescue and took youngest monster up for a blessing. It's a good job God's blessing overcame my thoughts or youngest daughter would have disappeared in a puff of smoke!

As the fidgeting and muttering about toilets was getting louder by the hour (it seemed like hours) I suggested that Elderly Relative Number One speak to the kind looking gentleman in the black frock hiding behind the hymn books at the back of the church. He said that the nearest toilets are in the town-centre – he might as well have said at the North Pole as, by this time, the situation, aggravated by the cold, was critical. Same kind gentleman, with great pity and sense of public duty, took elderly relative to toilet in a nearby house. Never did find out whose house it was as the occupants were in church at the time, but their dog looked a bit surprised!

Back home, fortified by a couple of gins, considerate husband who has been flying his radio controlled model 'planes all morning, oblivious to the stress I have been suffering, suggests that I should have a creative activity to help my nerves, and would I like to spend the next couple of years tramping round Bramshill Forest looking for the model 'plane he has managed to lose somewhere within a 50 mile radius.

I thank him for his solicitude and tell him what to do with his suggestion. He says I shouldn't shout virulent obscenities at him in front of the children. Nearly dislocating my jaw, I manage to convey my views to my spouse with great feeling, in a refined voice, and with a gracious smile.

Well, you at least have to appear to be enjoying yourself in front of slightly deaf elderly relatives, don't you, or else they mark you down as being only one step removed from the divorce courts.

But, of course, I like having elderly relatives to stay – doesn't everyone? I get my own back on them by putting them in the back seat of the car with dog, luggage and youngest child, and then drive round corners much too fast!

But when I see them off, I always say "Come again soon" and I can't be that bad, can I, because they always do"

THINGS THAT GO BUMP

Do you ever hear strange noises in the night? I could if only the dog would shut-up and let me listen! So I just lay there until I begin to feel quite sorry for my imaginary burglar.

First of all he'd have to get past our brainless hamster which thunders round on his exercise wheel if he hears anyone move in the night. This might be accomplished if the poor chap brought a few pounds of sunflower seeds along with his jemmy and wouldn't mind spending a couple of hours pushing them through the bars of the cage!

Then there's our hound. She'd be so delighted at the sight of company in the night that, ably abetted by the dog next door, she'd wake up half of Berkshire, tearing up and down the hall, trying to get our burglar to play ball!

And what about the problem of trying to creep round the house quietly. Well, most floors are covered with carpet – not ours. Ours is booby-trapped with roller skates on the stairs, airing racks of washing up the hall, and half completed model aeroplanes everywhere else. Not to mention the elderly relatives who descend on me frequently and deposit their camp beds wherever they can find a few feet of uncluttered space! Not easy obstacles to overcome in the dark.

Requests made to the inert body on my left to get himself downstairs to investigate is usually greeted with a spontaneous lack of enthusiasm.

Eventually, armed with my heaviest plastic vase, my fourteen-stone, six foot-two husband, whose ambition in life is to inflict nasty accidents on my imaginary burglars, takes himself and his bad temper downstairs to confront the intruder who, by this time, would have been reduced to a gibbering idiot and quivering with fear in the broom cupboard.

We're a very supportive family in times of crisis. Eldest daughter, clad in baby-doll pyjamas, now has one finger wedged in the nine on the extension 'phone, and youngest daughter adds to the chaos by appearing on the landing wearing her 'Wonder Woman' crown and shrieking "Hit him, Dad, hit him".

I don't know what a burglar would want in our house anyway. Everything in it is designed to give on the spot nervous breakdowns. The washing machine spends more time flooding the kitchen floor than it does washing, the cooker only cooks on one side, and it must be easier for an Eskimo to produce a cod fillet from beneath the North Pole than it is for me to hack through the ice in our freezer to extricate the fish fingers. But perhaps he would want our telly for its novelty value. All the people on it have green heads with red rings round them!

In fact, there's only one thing in our house that does actually work, and seeing her descending the stairs at three in the morning – like the avenging angel of death in a winceyette nightie – I don't think he'd want me!

WHAT'S UP DOC?

I must have a few virtues hidden away somewhere but I don't think patience and sympathy can be among them. All ailments, from bubonic plague to athletes' foot are treated the same in our house – with a pat on the head, a couple of aspirin and the words: "You'll feel better when you get there". Youngest daughter has long since given up on the old tummy ache routine on school spelling test days.

But this week I've really got my just desserts. Here I lay, totally ignored, with thumping head and aching joints – and do they care that I've got 'flu? – NO!

Sympathy from husband has amounted to: "You ought to see the doctor – his stock answer to all my problems which he relates, quite wrongly, to my hormones! But I'm too ill to go to the doctor and not ill enough for him to come to me.

Anyway, our doctor's so nice, he's the last person I want to see me looking like this. I never go to the doctor without first getting my best frock out of mothballs and putting three coats of paint on my face to cover my pasty complexion, and then sit in his chair apologising for being there, and telling him: "Yes, I'm very well, thank-you". In fact he's probably got me marked down on a secret file as being quite demented and a prime candidate for the nearest asylum!

There they all are – feeding their faces – and here I lay starving. When they eventually ask, I reply that I'd just like a little 'something light'. Now, what does 'a little something light' mean to you – a small portion of poached fish, a lightly boiled egg, a few grapes? Oh, No, not to my lot! They disappear for the next three hours and return in triumph with a cut-price, dented tin of some obscure brand of revolting Irish Stew and a pound of cooking apples!

And now, without me there bleating about TV violence, they're all downstairs avidly watching every picture designed to insult the intelligence of a backward hamster that flashes across the TV screen.

And here I stand, shivering on the landing, clutching my cold hot-water bottle to my crumpled winceyette, weakly calling for more aspirin and hot lemon – "And if someone doesn't come and dust this bedroom soon you'll need an excavator to dig me out!"

What do they do? They turn Starsky and Hutch up another hundred decibels so they can't hear me anymore. It's only the dog that loves me!

But now here's another day. At least, it's getting light so I suppose it's another day. Eldest daughter has just come into the bedroom. "Mum, I've got a sore throat, do you want to feel my glands?" "No, dear, (pat pat), have a couple of aspirin, you'll feel better when you get there".

Gosh, I'm back to normal, in fact, I feel well enough to enjoy laying here being ill today!

DEUTSCHEMARKS
AND DUCK-TAPE

Oh God! Here we go again. "Let's go on holiday", he says. "We can take the caravan". Whoopee! Another two weeks in a tin box with daughters arguing over who has the top bunk. To be fair, it's a nice little caravan – a Sprite Alpine we bought for £350 second-hand some years ago. At least it's ours now since we finished paying for it. It's got this Elsan Porta-Potti toilet that you put blue fluid in. Sometimes it splashes up when you're driving along and you get a blue ring round your bottom when you sit on the seat. It wears off – given time!

Husband has spent the last three days fitting a water pump so that cold water comes out of the tap when I pump the rubber button on the floor with my foot. In reality, what actually happens is, I press the foot pump up and down several times with no result; then, in frustration, I give it a good stamp and water spurts out with such velocity that everything is soaked within a three foot radius and nearly drowns me! Anyway, he's happy with the result and a tap with running water in the 'van will be useful even though it's cold. Still, I've got a nice gas ring and a shiny kettle that whistles!

Happy Campers

42

"Where do you want to go?" I ask. "We can't go back to France – they hate us there. Remember last year – getting the caravan stuck on the hairpin bend up some snow covered Alp?" We had to un-hitch the 'van, reverse the car and, with all of us pushing and shoving, physically turn the 'van round on a narrow hairpin bend high up a mountain, with a vertiginous drop on one side and the threat of an avalanche of snow covered boulders crashing down on the other.

After heaving the thing round for what seemed like hours, and with every sinew at breaking point, we achieved our object and re-coupled it to the car to drive back. But … the mountain road is just a single track with a few passing places … and we've blocked it!

That's when 'The French Incident' occurred! There's a queue of French drivers lined up either side of us in both directions. Chaos followed with drivers trying to reverse, horns blaring, fists shaking. I don't know much French but I did catch the words *"Anglais – Imbécile"*.

"OK, OK, not France. Let's go to Germany", he says. Personally I'd rather go to a nice little boarding house in Bognor. "We could go to the Black Forest or camp near the Rhine". The only Black Forest I want to see is a gateau bearing that name sitting squarely on a plate in front of me.

Youngest daughter, nearly seven – going on seventeen, and eldest daughter, just ten and already practising to be a stroppy teenager in her flared trousers and tank-top, both back him up, and so, here we are, packing the 'van to go to Germany. Eldest daughter insists on laying the 'swing-ball' along the length of the caravan for us all to trip over and youngest daughter starts the 'I'm having the top bunk' argument before we even leave home.

Husband, face puce and perspiring, is fitting the Calor gas bottle up and filling the tank with water for the journey. I make sure I pack essential things like washing power, diarrhoea mixture, my rubber gloves and a million tins of baked beans.

I'm quite lucky, I suppose, I have a 'cold' box, bright pink it is, and I put sachets of some frozen liquid in between the food to keep it cold on the journey; you know, things like bacon, butter, cheese and milk. It works quite well really – it keeps everything cold for a couple of days before the risk of food poisoning sets in.

So, Germany, like it or not, here we come. But ... first we have to negotiate the South Circular and get across London. Weaving through London traffic towing a caravan is a challenge at the best of times. We're doing reasonably well really until the traffic lights turn to red and we come to an abrupt stop. Unfortunately, the van behind us is a bit slow on the brake and, crash, bang, wallops into us. I can't tell you the chaos this causes in the heart of the London rush-hour.

With the shell of the caravan split apart at the outer corner, the rear lights shattered, and the Elsan Porta Potti clearly on show when peering through the space separating the side of the 'van from the back, this does not bode well! Husband sticks yards of duck-tape over the crack to hold it together and I paint red nail polish on the naked rear light bulbs. The Elsan toilet slops most of its blue fluid over the floor of the 'van and I get down on my hands and knees to try to mop it up. So now, here I am, with blue hands and matching blue knees! With the determination only possessed by mad Brits, we continue our journey.

So, here we are, two days later in the heart of Germany. We've no food, except for baked beans, as one of the frozen fluid bags burst, depositing an ammonia smelling gunge all over the food rendering it inedible.

"Let's go swimming", suggests youngest daughter. I'm up for that, we've not washed properly for two days and we could all get clean. Perhaps the chlorine in the pool will bleach the blue colour out of my hands and knees! Husband, who hates water and can't swim, moans and groans a bit, but concedes we ought to let the children go swimming; we are on holiday after all. And, there in a nice little town called Baden-Breisig Something or Other, is a *Hallenbad* which, after consulting the German dictionary, we translate as meaning 'indoor swimming-pool'. And in we go. It's spotlessly clean and completely empty. There are two doors, one labelled *Herren* and one labelled *Damen*. Now, our German is non-existent and we've left the dictionary in the 'van so, taking a bit of a chance, husband disappears through the *Herren* door and daughters and I proceed through the door marked *Damen*.

We have the whole place to ourselves; nobody asks for any money and the swimming pool is a delight. We get into our cossies and, as we're all alone, husband joins us in the *Damen* section through an inter-connecting door. And then SHE, the Commandant, appears. I don't know what she is shouting but she's in a frenzy about something. I try a smile of appeasement – I think Neville Chamberlain tried that some

45

forty years ago – it didn't do him much good either! Husband, standing there in his plastic 'jelly' sandals with the rusty buckles, maroon bri-nylon bathing trunks with the ladder in them, and a bright orange rubber cap which is so tight it's pulled his head into a funny shape with one ear sticking out, is riveted to the spot. I conclude that the shrieking is because husband is in the *Damen* section wearing his shoes.

The Commandant, bosoms heaving in a giant *büstenhalter*, looking suspiciously at my blue knees (I hide my hands behind my back), marshals us into the pool and husband creeps in to join us. He doesn't actually swim; he just stands in the shallow end and moans a lot as we splash about. The beady eyes in the podgy face of our Teutonic 'Guardian of the Pool' follow our every splash. No wonder there's nobody else here – she's scary!

Finally we get out of the water and, with quivering hostility, she demands money to pay for a pristine towel on which we are instructed to dry ourselves. I'm ashamed to say I remove the rest of the blue staining on my body on her white towel, but I fold it over so she can't see. This 'dragon-in-charge', her ample proportions still menacing, keeps a close watch on husband who is now displaying a bright red indentation around his forehead from wearing the tight orange rubber cap. And ... I'm sure one of his ears is now stuck at a funny angle. Still muttering threats she ushers us all out of the door. Daughters and I are in hysterics when we get back to the 'van and husband is the first one to hit the aspirin bottle.

"Let's eat out tonight", says husband. I'm all for that seeing as we haven't got any food anyway. We're camped in a beautiful spot just a five minute walk from the River Rhine, at a place called Freis-Eisle Something Glupk. Anyway, it's very nice, so off we go to look for somewhere to eat. And there it is – on the water's edge, a beautiful little restaurant, all wood and cuckoo clocks, so in we go. Big Mistake!

After agonising over the menu which we don't understand a word of – there's obviously nothing with chips – we decide to each order something different as we can share out whatever they serve; there's bound to be something we like. Wrong! A plate of odd coloured cabbage is the first thing to arrive, followed by weird smelling sausages. The gateau we have for pudding is wonderful. We should have had three helpings of that and not bothered with the rest. I think we'll stick to baked beans next time.

But now – big problem; they've presented us with the bill. It's astronomical and we don't have enough deutschemarks! I wonder if they'll let me go back to the caravan to get my rubber gloves if they make us wash-up. But, of course, why are we panicking? We can write a travellers' cheque – problem solved. Oh Yeah! We can fill in the figures but how do you write the amount in words? And what's German for August? After much consultation of the dictionary, which I have cleverly decided will never leave my side again after the swimming pool episode, we manage. Until – "Who do we make the cheque payable to?" queries husband. Well, it's obvious, there, on the top of the bill still quivering in his hand, is the name of whoever owns the restaurant – *'Trink Bohlar'*. So the cheque is duly made out to *'Trink Bohlar'* and passed to a sniggering waiter. I don't know what's so funny but he shows it to another waiter and they both disappear through a door at the back of the room. We decide to do a runner at this stage.

Walking back along the River Rhine, I'm amazed to see all the restaurants are called *'Trink Bohlar'*. Grabbing the dictionary we discover it's an advertisement for beer. So now, somewhere in the German banking system, is our travellers' cheque made payable to 'Drink Beer'. Daughters are almost collapsing with laughter, me, mildly hysterical, not to mention a bit wobbly after two glasses of wine (I'm not used to drinking wine) and husband is contemplating throwing himself in the river.

Now, back at the caravan, here I am, mopping up more blue fluid oozing from the Elsan toilet, and gazing at the moon through the crack in the wall. What's duck-tape in German? I wonder if we've got enough deutschemarks to buy some more tomorrow.

I expect the Germans all hate us now as well!

*Author's note: Is it **Duct** or **Duck Tape**? I don't want to cause confusion, so I will clarify. The first name for Duct Tape was DUCK. During World War II the U.S. Military needed a waterproof tape to keep the moisture out of ammunition cases. So, they enlisted the Johnson and Johnson Permacel Division to manufacture the tape. Because it was waterproof, everyone referred to it as 'duck' tape (like water off a duck's back). Military personnel discovered that the tape was good for lots more than keeping out water. They used it for Jeep repairs, fixing stuff on their guns, strapping equipment to their clothing ... the list is endless. It's quite good for the temporary repair of caravans too!*

JUST ONE OF THOSE DAYS

Do you have days when you know the safest thing to do would be to go back to bed and stay there? You know, the sort of day when you dash into work, fling off your coat, and find yourself standing in the middle of the office wearing your pinny!

I should have known the other day was going to be like that when I found my shower cap floating in the loo. Oh well, wet tendrils of hair can always be wound round a couple of curlers.

The hub-bub below sounded reassuringly normal. Daughters were arguing over whose turn it was to take the dog to the nearest lamp-post and back. Husband, trying to assemble cheese sandwiches, was complaining about jam and Marmite smeared liberally all over the bread-board. It's lovely – you can't hear a thing under the shower!

Out of the shower, I realise things are hotting up down below. Husband enquires, mildly hysterically I thought, if I expect him to go to work with his pyjama top tucked into his trousers as he can't find a clean shirt. I refrain from telling him that I don't care if he tucks his pyjamas into a loin cloth and goes to work, and concentrate constructively on the feasibility of rubbing talcum powder into the grubby marks on the neck of yesterday's shirt.

A bang and a shriek from downstairs send us all flying to the kitchen where eldest daughter has managed to explode her Thermos flask by pouring boiling water on to the tea-bag that has been wedged in the bottom of it for the last three days.

We decide not to try to pick the million fragments of glass out of the Marmite / Jam / Cheese sandwiches, and sandwich making starts in earnest all over again.

I suppose I really ought to get this sandwich making business organised. Eldest daughter only likes Marmite; youngest daughter only likes jam (the puce coloured homemade variety – unset and soaking-in-the-bread type); and husband only likes cheese.

Tonight I'll make up six months' supply, stack them in the freezer, and then slap two rounds of frozen bread on their upturned palms every morning as they file out through the back door. Me – I just settle for a Mars bar.

Finally, husband, having located his brief-case under the hamster's cage, takes eldest daughter off to the local comprehensive, and I pack youngest daughter into the car to go to her junior school. In a few more minutes I shall be able to creep into my warm, cosy office and, well hidden by the typewriter, drift contentedly through the day.

"Mum", pipes up a voice from the back, totally shattering my reverie, "Why are you going to work with those two curlers in the back of your hair ….?"

ALL IN A DAY'S WORK

Did you have a nice Christmas? I did, I think. As a school secretary Christmas for me starts in September when I am still mentally on holiday. The habitual harassed expression teachers wear is replaced by one of frenzy and, again this year, I was dragged from my hiding place behind the typewriter to help with the shopping for Father Christmas.

This year's outing had the added joy of a two-hour sight-seeing tour of the roadworks on the motorway. At the warehouse I show true grit and determination when, clutching my calculator in one hand, half a ton of tinsel, plasticine and advent calendars in the other, I am persuaded up a wobbly ladder to secure the exact shade of red crepe paper required for some obscure project, and risk braining myself when the whole lot comes tumbling down!

If we ever get back to school I must remember to remain hidden for the next three months because every time I pause I'm given wrapping paper, sellotape, and meaningful looks! I wonder if I could pay NALGO for protection from this sort of thing.

Every organisation has its Scrooge and we're no exception. Our Scrooge is the Department of Education which does not recognise Christmas. Relentlessly each Monday morning a sack full of forms and directives and other useless rubbish arrives in the office. And what happens when I have spent hours compiling highly sophisticated statistical data, in triplicate, about how many children eat Brussels sprouts and how many bottles of milk have been drunk in school in the last fifty years, and place it for signature – well, I'll tell you –

51

it gets covered up with piles of Christmas cards, paper chains and plates of gunge which arrive in rapid succession ready for the Christmas parties. Worse still, it gets irretrievably lost amongst the wrapping paper only to emerge again around March when everybody has forgotten why on earth it was done in the first place.

Party days arrive – at least it's easy to know what to wear on those days – you just enquire as to the colour of the jelly and wear something that matches. After tea has been well coughed and spluttered over, and partially eaten, Father Christmas, a very brave man, faces a horde of excited children waiting for their presents to be produced from his sack. Meanwhile the press gang have organised helpers to clear up the disaster area which was formerly the school dining room.

As the last needle falls off the tree Christmas chaos finishes at school and starts at home. Christmas Eve morning arrives along with the mob of elderly relatives whom I invited during a weak moment when Christmas was a long way off.

I decide that we would all enjoy going to the children's afternoon church service to set the atmosphere for Christmas. We arrive three hours early and, after playing musical chairs in the pews for a while, I find myself seated in the front row where I think the choir boys normally sit.

And how do you refrain elderly male relative, full of bonhomie and liquid lunch-time Christmas spirit, from clapping and saying "Well done" after every reading? At least their voices added volume, if not quality, to the singing, although I've never heard 'The First Noel' sung to the tune of

'Good King Wenceslas' before. As the children want to make Christingles to enhance the tea table when we get home, I just concentrate on praying that if I provide the paraphernalia they won't set fire to the decorations.

I enjoyed going to a party on Christmas Eve and, arriving home in a happy mood in the early hours, found that the sacks left for Father Christmas had been baited with cow bells in the bottom and tied to respective big toes. Woman's Lib be blowed! – I left Father Christmas to sort that one out for himself and steeled myself ready for the 6.30 a.m. onslaught when I would be required to admire all the gifts that he had brought.

Christmas morning proceeds and all the neighbours come in, bringing with them their elderly relatives and children. After a couple of quick gins, they went home muttering something about a turkey in the oven, leaving the elderly relatives behind to turn my sitting room into something resembling an old folks' community rest home!

After an exhausting half-hour of shouting at the old who are deaf and can't hear and the young who are deaf and won't hear, I overcame their spontaneous lack of enthusiasm and returned them to their rightful owners.

Boxing Day afternoon was fun too. I spent it unclogging the Hoover which was bunged up with walnut shells and half a satsuma!

But now it's all over for another year. I'm told you only really enjoy Christmas when the children are young and, watching my eldest daughter in front of the mirror curling her hair with a heated thing Granny gave her, I don't have many more to enjoy.

But what can you say when your youngest puts her arms around your neck and says "Oh Mum, isn't Christmas smashing. I wish it was Christmas every day". You have to say "Yes, love, so do I".

SOAPBOX

Are you a constant source of embarrassment to your off-spring? I know I am, but sometimes I have to stand on my soapbox and scream and shout. Usually nobody listens to me, insignificant as I am, but there are some things in life that really matter and then all the world has to know about it, however unpopular it makes me.

And what I'm in a tizzy about is the emotive issue of hunting … so, somebody help me up onto my wobbly soapbox so that I can beat the tambourine on the subject of fox-hunting or the hunting of any live quarry.

Fortunately, most of us have progressed far enough along the trail of civilisation to abhor violence of any kind, but sadly, and frighteningly, there still exists an element of evil within our society where pleasure and excitement is derived from the killing and torturing of animals.

This not only applies to fox hunting, but to all forms of pitting animals against each other, be they hounds against fox, hawk against sparrow, matador against bull. (Yes, a matador is an animal in my book).

The exploitation of animals for the sheer amusement of man is a medieval and dangerous trait and I can't bear it.

Whether or not the fox population has to be culled will have to be left to the experts. Whether they are killed with pleasure or regret is a matter for everyone's conscience.

Perhaps one day in the future somebody will listen to the hysterical rantings of a soft-hearted house-wife. Until then, somebody get me down off this bloody soapbox before I break my neck!

THE NOT SO WISE BROWN OWL

Did you have a nice holiday? I did, I think! Being a school secretary I'm obliged to endure longer holidays than anyone else and, as I'm a bit of a 'do-gooder', and not wanting to waste my spare time, I decided to take my Brownies on Pack Holiday.

You didn't know that in addition to being a school secretary, part-time writer, and full-time general dogsbody, I'm a 'Brown Owl' as well, did you?

Have you ever tried packing enough equipment to keep twenty energetic little girls amused for the best part of a week?

I started off on the wrong foot when, at 6.30 a.m., I persuaded my husband, who thinks I'm mad anyway, to help shove a ton of luggage, enough to fill an articulated truck, into the boot, back seat, front seat, and every other available inch of space, of my long suffering little Allegro.

He will keep putting the trunks in before I've finished packing them and I end up with plastic carrier bags full of vital equipment like toilet rolls, diarrhoea mixture and glue all rolling around the floor of the car!

Promptly at 8.45 a.m. my three press-ganged helpers arrived and, fortified by a cup of tea and an aspirin sandwich, we drove off in convoy muttering "Never Again!"

Mid-day found us buried in a village hall in the heart of the countryside waiting for the first Brownie to arrive looking angelic and slightly overawed – a state which I know from past experience, never lasts for long!

First night away was pretty peaceful – we only got up nine times, which compares favourably with the twenty-seven times we got up on the first night of our last pack holiday.

All parents will recognise the phrases, "Mum, I want a drink of water", "Mum, I want to go to the toilet", "Mum, there's a spider up here", when children are in bed. Just multiply that by twenty and substitute 'Brown Owl' for 'Mum' and you'll realise that Guiders never expect to actually go to sleep themselves on Pack Holiday anyway.

During our week away we were visited by a senior Guider. The Brownies, thoughtful as ever, invited her to stay for tea and enhanced her enjoyment of the meal by gargling with the tea and spluttering all over her cheese-on-toast. I'm surprised my Pack Holiday Licence wasn't revoked on the spot.

The week progressed: we played rounders with the local lads – we won, of course, because Brownies are never out – they just join the end of the batting queue again. We went to the zoo, saw the chimps having their tea. And Brown Owl thinks it's much more fun paddling in the sea in wellies because she doesn't have to dig out all that nasty wet sand from between two-hundred toes.

Lastly the midnight feast and then it was time for us all to pack our kit-bags and come home. If you saw a convoy of four cars weaving their way up the A30 last Thursday evening, with exhausted haggard drivers at the wheels – it was us!

And home again – "Good Grief, you look shattered", says husband before disappearing to the local chippy to beg for his dinner. "What you need is a holiday".

So, here I am, having spent the best part of last night packing the caravan, sitting in a field behind a cow-shed, with the wind blowing in the wrong direction, with the dog, hamster, and two stick-insects for company.

Daughters have gone off to help with the milking, husband has gone on a three-mile hike in search of water, and I just sit here praying for the stamina to hold on for another week until I can get back to my hiding place behind the typewriter, and continue to fill in forms, in triplicate, of course, for the dear old Department of Education!

FLOWERS THAT BLOOM

Are all school secretaries as lucky or as gullible as me? For the second time running I was persuaded that I would love to give up a morning in a comfortable office for the delights of a day at Kew in the June sunshine. An apprehensive nod was taken as agreement and my fate sealed. Please Mr. Weatherman, don't drown me again this year – he didn't listen, did he!

The chosen day dawned, or rather lurked, shrouded in fine rain and mist. Mental note: Put sun-dress back in wardrobe – take out plastic mac, umbrella, trousers and wellies! Pack aspirin, sick pills, tissues and sick bucket – Kew here I come!

Teachers don't listen either, do they? I particularly asked just to be put in charge of a couple of quiet, gentle children who would treat me kindly throughout the day. I was given five who somehow didn't quite fit that category but, undeterred, we all got on the coach, waved goodbye, and I swallowed the first sick pill.

We had an uneventful journey, feet stuck firmly to the floor with Coke leaking from leak-proof Tupperware, and a boiled sweet stuck on the elbow of my plastic mac.

Kew Gardens is beautiful – I think! I didn't actually see very much of it. Keeping track of five children is something like painting the Forth Bridge – by the time you've counted No. 5 you've lost No. 1 again. I did see Kew Gardens toilets though (all of them) frequently.

Most of the children carried, or wanted me to carry, a suitcase full of food which had the unfortunate habit of breaking open, distributing pots of yoghurt and Granny Smith's liberally over the herbaceous borders.

Lunch, enough to feed the proverbial 5,000, was shared with the ducks and me! My five, anxious to keep my strength up, fed me a variety of crisps, fish-paste sandwiches, and bits of chocolate with finger prints on them. All much appreciated. Well, I did share my umbrella with them.

The heavens opened. Thank-you God for cedar trees in Kew Gardens. We all got under one. Some dear child, concerned that we might get waterlogged and never move again, suggested we might like to make a three-mile dash to the Palm House. I don't know why I listened; I couldn't even see the Palm House through the rain, but I think I enjoyed it as, nearly falling over the balcony, I tried to hold on to the backs of anoraks while my lot held a shrieking conversation with friends hundreds of feet below.

I dutifully assisted with the purchasing of postcards for every relative in Berkshire and then, huddled together under the umbrella, we paddled back to the coach.

Oh God – there's one missing from my group! One, two, three … four??? Panic! Where's No. 5. Decide to delay my nervous breakdown until I had strangled No. 5 with her anorak cord! I expect that group of Australians still talk about a mad woman running through the rhododendrons looking for a child who was still calmly buying yet another postcard.

At last we're back on the coach: we wring out skirts, plimsolls, and hair. I know I'm still in one piece as my head is thumping twice a second to remind me. And thank-you, that kind Mum who made me a cup of tea when I got back.

I went on to meet my own little girl from school. "Mummy", she said, "You are lucky, our school secretary isn't allowed to go on school outings". I wonder if I'll be allowed to go next year.

HAPPY DAYS AND HOLIDAYS

Well, I can't believe all this biased ranting I've just heard on the radio. Some talk-show hosted by a charmless bloke who hates caravans (and their occupants) and obviously doesn't know how to enjoy himself. What's he got against caravans? I bet he hasn't even stayed in one. He's drivelling on about caravans only being allowed on the road between twelve mid-night and six in the morning!

We never speed – our 'van travels at no more than twenty-five miles an hour and that's quite fast enough on any motorway. When it comes to country lanes, we tuck in nicely between tractors and horse-boxes so nobody could overtake even if they wanted to.

Anyway – practical issues determine our holidays. When we go away, along with daughters Number One and Number Two, we are accompanied by the dog, the hamster, and two stick-insects. Hotels – I'm dreaming again – we can't afford hotels – I should say Boarding House landladies aren't too keen when I walk in clutching a gold-fish bowl housing Lucrezia and Horace, our two stick-insects. They're quite harmless and no trouble, just a body about three inches long with six legs ... and antennae.

I acquired them from the school where I work as a secretary. We had lots and they like to breed! Well, what species doesn't! Stick-insects need something to do when they're stuck in a glass cage. Anyway, during one fateful, never to be forgotten, Parents' Evening some dear little junior knocked the glass tank to the floor and, amid the shattered fragments, out crawled a million stick-inserts. Some must have been

63

teenagers let loose for the first time – on rampaging legs they careered across the room, up the stairs and along the corridor to the hall, with me, as a dutiful school secretary, in pursuit.

Have you ever tried to gather up a multitude of baby stick-insects before they invade 'Parents' Evening' and everybody starts screaming or, worse, treading on them? To my ever-lasting shame, not helped by the hilarity displayed by teachers who should know better, and wresting the broom from the caretaker before he swept them into oblivion, my rescue effort was only partially successful. In a placatory gesture in order to keep my job, I adopted Lucrezia and Horace.

Having denied Lucrezia and Horace the diversity of livening up Parents' Evening I offered them very nice accommodation in our spare bedroom causing untold stress to elderly relatives who have to share the spare room. In fact, Elderly Relative Number One insists on getting undressed in the bathroom as she says Horace watches her. And Elderly Relative Number Two refuses point-blank to steal privet from next-door's hedge on which I feed them; so that's down to me too!

Our stick-insects enjoy a rampant sex-life. Each day I clean out hundreds of little pin-head size eggs and dispose of them. I couldn't 'dispose' of them once they'd hatched and don't want a Babylonian plague of stick-insects munching their way through the Brussels sprouts mouldering in the larder.

So, here we are, off to take an early Spring break, in a car that's replaced the one that's been written off, towing the caravan in a somewhat erratic manner, to the Isle of Wight. Why erratic? Well, let me tell you.

At the beginning of the week, I'm nicely ensconced watching early-evening telly, potatoes bubbling merrily into a mush for our dinner, when the vague thought crosses my befuddled brain that husband is late. And then comes the 'phone call. It's P.C. Plod from the Police Station saying in an irritatingly calm voice that he is sorry to tell me that my husband has been injured in a car accident and taken to the local hospital. I hate people who are calm when I feel galloping hysteria taking over! That is the moment when your heart lurches.

Leaving a hastily scribbled note for daughters and hoping they have their keys (I admit they're 'latch-key kids' – I have to go out to work to help pay the mortgage and eldest is nearly a teenager now) I get into my little Allegro and rush off to the hospital where I finally locate him in a side cubicle surrounded by doctors, nurses, and two policemen.

There is he, propped up, with a broken arm, a gaping wound in his side and a broken nose, muttering incoherently, with a face resembling a tomato that somebody has trodden on. They only let me in to see him after I assured them I wasn't squeamish and that he wasn't a pretty sight at the best of times!

A week later, in a replacement car and undaunted by circumstances, here we go, weaving our way to the Isle of Wight; husband has his nose all bunged up with gauze, has strapping around his middle, and his left arm in a plaster-cast. And he won't let me drive because we're towing the 'van! Why are men so stubborn? We actually jointly drive

65

the car; he steers with one hand and depresses the clutch and, on his command, I change gear. We manage quite well really and arrive on the Isle of Wight unscathed. First thing in the morning we must locate the local hospital to have the gauze up his nose changed. What a way to start a holiday. But … I am allowed to drive now we're not towing the caravan.

Next comes putting up the awning and daughters, dog and I set to with more desperation than enthusiasm and a complete lack of skill, with husband bawling out instructions. Hamster and stick-insects are not much help at this stage. But, it's getting dark, blowing a gale and starting to rain. With acres of canvas and hundreds of poles to fit together in a, by now, howling gale, it's not easy. And … if husband doesn't stop shouting at us soon (we're doing our best and it's not our fault the dog's run off and buried the tent pegs) I'm going to garrotte him with the guy ropes!

We somehow survive a leaky seven days mopping up puddles as I've failed miserably to properly connect the caravan to the awning which is spending the week madly flapping in the wind and threatening to take us airborne at any moment. It's not all bad – we have to go to the hospital every other day, where it's nice and warm and dry, having plaster-cast checked and gauze shoved up and down husband's broken nose. Every holiday has its highlights!

Now, a year on, it's "Let's go back to France again". Well, we can't go to Spain, we upset them last year – the Spanish all hate us now! There we were, on this really nice, quite large camping-site in hot sun-shine, (from which I'm always trying to find shade as it brings me out in a rash) and he sets up the barbecue. Having spent hours finding bits of twigs and piling half a ton of charcoal on top, it's time to light up. Will the thing light? In your dreams! We have the remains of two different types of barbecue lighter fluid lurking in bottles in the 'van – "Let's chuck them on to get it going" he says. With sausages and burgers of suspicious Spanish origin, curling at the edges and starting to pulsate, I'm happy to agree to anything. The dregs of the first bottle is emptied on with little effect. Then the contents remaining in the second bottle follow. Big mistake! What happens next is a chemical reaction on the scale of atomic testing over Bikini Island.

Billowing grey and yellow smoke engulf the entire camp-site causing a mass evacuation! Caravans and tents are abandoned and the site owner has an apoplectic fit. Burgers and sausages are disposed of, we lock ourselves in our 'van, go to bed hungry, and leave before anybody gets up the next morning. No, we can't go back to Spain!

So, France it is this year. "Let's be really adventurous and tow the caravan down to the South of France" he says. And … here we are, camped on a nice big site (it even has a launderette but the Germans seem to have commandeered that) right by the beautiful blue Med. We're not risking a charcoal barbecue this year. We've a lovely new electric barbecue and this site is so up-market we can connect into the electricity supply – how's that for all mod-cons. No burgers on this little beauty – we've got salmon would you believe! I've never cooked salmon before – it's too expensive – but I've wrapped it in foil and prepared a lovely salad to go with it. Daughters don't like salad – they eat baked beans with everything.

Come dusk, with the moon rising over the ocean, cicadas chirping, the scene set with candles, we switch on our barbecue. Oh Yes – you've guessed – another Big Mistake! The barbecue takes ten watts and each camping emplacement only has an allocation of six! Well, the hissing, sparking and crackling, followed by a big bang, is heard all over the camp-site. We can't hide from the fact that it is husband – the *'Anglais Imbécile'* – who has plunged the entire camp-site into darkness as every electrical appliance shudders to an abrupt stop. Every light fuses and there is a suspicious smell of burning from the sockets from all the caravans around us. There is a plus though – the washing machines in the launderette have stopped – the Germans are hopping mad, unable to extract their various *büstenhalters* and whatever other *unterwäsche* they want to wear in the foreseeable future.

I wonder what country we can inflict ourselves on next year?

BACK TO SCHOOL

Now, it's not that I don't love my daughters dearly, because I do, but I bet I'm not the only parent in Berkshire who sighs with relief at the end of the school holidays.

We've been through the argument in the shoe shop over what shoes I consider sensible to start back to school in and what shoes eldest daughter thinks she's going to be allowed to get away with.

And youngest daughter has been advised emphatically that I have no intention of getting up at 4.0 a.m. in order to sort her hair into three million plaits with beads on the ends of them so that she can go to school looking like a refugee just to impress other nine year olds!

"You haven't signed my school report", admonishes eldest daughter, "and, what's more, you're not to write any comments on it again this year!" Me … comment … as if I would!

But there was one report that had me struck dumb with admiration. 'Her knitting has improved', it said. As I've been trying to teach her to knit for the last ten years, anyone achieving this feat would, in my opinion, deserve a medal for sheer grit and determination.

"What, for Heaven's sake, have you knitted?" I ask in amazement. "Can't remember", was the unenlightening reply. "Perhaps they mean my crochet". "But you did most of that at home in bed", I said.

"Perhaps they mean the skirt I made", suggested eldest daughter helpfully. "Nice try, dear" – it was, in fact, a pretty good first effort – and by the time I'd unpicked the hem, re-done the zip, and sorted out the waist-band – Oxfam was delighted with it.

I persevered – "Show me what you can do". Just a few rows in garter stitch didn't seem too great a feat for someone who has 'improved'.

Three hours later, with the wool in a tangled muddle of knots on the floor and the knitting needles bent at odd angles, I asked what the problem was. "Well, I can do garter stitch", she assured me, "it's just that I've forgotten how to cast on!"

I must remind her to try harder this term though. I don't think I could face the stigma if it was reported to me that her knitting had deteriorated!

THE DISHWASHER

I've never been one to cultivate friendships for any ulterior motive, but if you see an advert in the 'Personal' column saying: 'Deserted housewife wishes to meet friendly plumber', it will be me!

Now, I may be bit naïve, but I thought dishwashers were supposed to wash dishes. Not ours! Ours has stood smugly gleaming in the corner of the kitchen, having had loving glances lavished upon it, and polished twice daily, for the past three weeks, and here I stand, day after day, up to my armpits, with greasy washing-up water slopping over the tops of my rubber gloves, causing permanently crinkled hands. All except Sundays that is, when husband assembles elderly relatives around the sink to spend a jolly afternoon scouring the three hundred pans that I have used to cook dinner in.

Now, my other half knows as much about Do-It-Yourself as I know about deep sea diving, and anything I want done yesterday takes him at least ten years to do.

For the past decade our loo door has been a constant source of embarrassment to elderly relatives as the door won't stay shut unless you keep your foot up against it. By now, I must have the only acrobatic relatives in the district. In fact, some have reached a peak of agility they never knew they possessed all because of our loo door!

But back to the dishwasher. Due to my constant complaints, for the past week all I've seen of my other half is his rear end sticking out from the cupboard under the sink as he endeavours to become better acquainted with the intricacies of the pipes and wires protruding from the contraption.

All attempts at conversation have been met with monosyllabic answers, except that is, for the frequent outbursts of unmentionable expletives and howls of anguish!

Anyway, last night, well actually in the early hours of this morning, I was informed that it was 'all systems go', and I could finally load the dishwasher with the three days dirty dishes I had been vindictively storing up for its opening performance.

A quick read of the instructions was all that was necessary. "Where's the salt", asks haggard looking husband. "What salt?" says me. Well, did you know that dishwashers require feeding with half a ton of salt before they operate? My feeble shakes of the salt cellar did little to relieve the ominous atmosphere of doom which descended on the kitchen and all within it. These new-fangled gadgets are obviously a bit beyond me!

And so, here I stand, at two in the morning, up to my armpits etc., and there, sound asleep and undisturbed, stands the dishwasher.

But my turn will come! All I need is a ton of salt and a friendly plumber .....

AN IDEAL DAY OUT

Have you ever tried strap-hanging on the Tube clutching a chip-pan, surrounded by hundreds of football hooligans? It's all the fault of my two friends who seem to think I should be included in their masochistic activities.

"Do you want to come to the Ideal Home Exhibition?" says a bright voice on the 'phone. Seeing as I'm completely lacking in the art of house-wifery, and my home could only be described as 'lived-in' when looking its best, I expect they thought the experience would do me good.

A ticket, bought at Winnersh Station, took us painlessly to Earls Court and into the exhibition. I couldn't actually see the exhibits because the three of us were immediately jammed into a throng of writhing bodies as we fought our way from one stand to the next. Talk about survival of the fittest! We didn't fight for long as a three hour wait for the loo took up a good bit of the day.

After a dubious lunch of slightly warm potted meat sandwiches eaten squatting on the floor of the double glazing stand, we decided on a cup of tea. We descended into a dive snowed under with the rubbish of millions who had passed that way before us and, cooling our elbows in others people's tea slops, we were revived with a plastic cup of hot water, complete with floating tea bag, and a frozen cake – so frozen we had to lick it like a lolly!

I can only relate the experience as akin to torture, except perhaps that would have been a darn sight less painful and somewhat cheaper than the jaw-dropping amount we were charged.

But what about the chip-pan? Well, you have to buy something at these places and I did need one. "Will it go in the dishwasher?" I ask the glib salesman busily smoking all over the beef burgers. "Yes" he says. "Are you sure?" I ask. With a look that I will describe politely as 'withering' he emphatically assured me it could go in a hundred dishwashers. And so I became the owner of the chip-pan.

Our journey home was the experience of a lifetime. Do the trains only run on a Saturday for the supporters of some football team called Chelsea? Or do any normal people ever travel on that day? We maintained terrified silence as we thundered through the tunnels in the company of tattooed hooligans wearing ear-rings and blue and white stripped scarves and who seemed to converse in a language completely alien to English as we know it.

In addition my chip-pan and I were riveted by the amazing sight of two female members of the species with orange cheeks and purple hair. And, you won't believe this, one had a ring through the side of her nose!

At Bracknell Station a highly inebriated character resembling Billy Bunter, in a grey woolly cardigan and a 'kiss-me-quick' hat, appeared at our carriage window and insisted in planting kisses on the glass. Although something for the three of us to laugh over afterwards – perhaps not so funny for a young girl travelling alone! And we're still wondering where on earth the other two drunks in the carriage with us ended up!

I never usually support the blackmail effect of strike action, but if British Rail employees have all this to put up with every Saturday not only would I support a strike in protest but, for two pins, I'd walk in front holding a banner!

And now I'm home – complete with chip-pan.   First instruction on the label – *'Never put in a dishwasher'.* And there in the kitchen the dishwasher marks up another notch thinking of me up to my armpits scouring the chip-pan. But I'm not in the mood to be trifled with! Sorry chip-pan, as much as I've appreciated your company during the perilous hours we've spent together on British Rail, you've been misrepresented and you're going back!

I wonder if those two friends would like another trip to London with me and my chip-pan again next Saturday!

FOUR GO ADVENTURING AGAIN

We've got this new caravan – well, it's not exactly new; if we're talking 'exactly', it's exactly quite a few years old, but it's new to us. And, you'll never believe this – it's got a cocktail cabinet with little glass doors. How's that for posh! I'm stocking that before we start thinking baked beans, diarrhoea mixture and clean knickers. First to go in is a dozen little bottles of Babycham – they're going at the front because they've pretty blue tops with a little dancing horse on them. I'm not taking our four Babycham glasses though – they'd only get broken. We'll stick to the plastic beakers. And – what else? – Oh yes, we've some Advocaat left over from Christmas – we'll take that too. I can make 'snowballs' with a cherry on the top. There's also an inch of sweet sherry lurking at the bottom of a bottle – not worth taking that so I'll drink it.

But where shall we go this year? Out comes the atlas. "How about Lake Constance in Germany? – We can go to Austria and Switzerland from there". It's a long way and we'd have to travel through France to get there – whoopee – we can upset most of the continent in one fell swoop if this comes about.

Husband, fired with enthusiasm, starts planning the route. "I could help with the driving, couldn't I?" I see his expression change. I'm not allowed to tow the caravan since one fateful journey on a motor-way in France which had a downhill gradient, and I drove too fast and we got into a 'snake'. The caravan swerved violently from side to side throwing everything inside all over the place. Apparently, if that happens you have to 'step on the gas' to pull it out of the snake. I'm not sure what I did but we managed to recover our equilibrium amid a lot of screaming and yelling. I wish I could say the same for the contents of the 'van – we were knee deep in blue Elsan toilet fluid and baked beans by the time we shuddered to a halt. No, I'm not allowed to tow the 'van now.

I just have to stick to the domestic routine of the caravan; you know – women's stuff – cleaning, packing, shopping, cooking – just like being at home really – hey-ho, my role in life. But I've got the washing down to a fine art – how's this for innovative? I have a big yellow bucket with a lid (it used to be the Napisan bucket when the children were babies and I had to soak the terry-towelling nappies in it before putting them in the washing machine). Anyway, I pile all the dirty clothes in it, fill it with water, add a handful of washing-powder, and slap on the lid good and tight. Then we leave it in the caravan as we drive along. The water is agitated by the movement of the 'van and all the clothes get clean – pure genius! Oh yes, I forgot to say in the previous paragraph – the yellow bucket tipped over during my 'snake' as well! What with the soapy water mixing with the blue Elsan toilet fluid we now have some very strange coloured underwear.

So, we're off, and it's where to spend the first night in France. As you know, I work as a school secretary and so have to endure six weeks of summer holidays. (I only got the job because the head-mistress liked me and I was truthful enough to say to the Governors that I wanted the job because of the holidays as I had two school age children – everyone else had lied apparently). But anyway, husband does not enjoy that luxury. He only has the statutory two weeks holiday each year. Well – it was him who said, "Let's start the journey immediately I get home from work – I'll try to get off early".

And we did, start off directly he came home from work I mean. Elderly relatives ensconced at home to look after cat, dog and stick insects, there was nothing to stop us driving off into the evening sunshine and get the ferry to France. No problem. Of course it's very late and pitch black when we get off the boat and start our journey along French roads heading south. At some point we have to stop for the night – but where? I'm frightened to stop at AutoRoute Service Stations – you hear dreadful tales of hi-jacking and robbers filling caravans with gas in those places so we just want to find some quiet spot and pull up for a few hours to sleep before driving on.

Finally we find an entrance along a little rough track. It's very uneven and absolutely pitch-black, but no problem, we find a clearing and settle down. We are awakened by the most God-Awful banging and clanging and revving of engines. I fearfully pull aside the curtains and nearly drop dead with shock. We're in the middle of a stone quarry with trucks all around us revving their engines and blaring their horns. Piles of quarried stone are mountainous all around us and I expect they are planning to plant explosives into the quarry sides towering above us. "Get dressed", I shriek at husband, "before they dynamite us".

This isn't the only time we've been in danger of being blown up – for some inexplicable reason I'm cross with him for getting us into this pickle. "Remember that time in Spain when the Basques were planting bombs under cars and I thought I could smell burning?" I had totally panicked and dragged the children out of the back of the car screaming at them to run before husband had actually even managed to do an emergency stop. I think I was in over-drive because some anti-Brit thug had smashed the car side windows when we'd left it in the supermarket car-park up the road. So, already on edge, the burning smell was the final straw to convince me they'd attached a bomb to the underside of the car.

So, with husband determined to do all the driving, on we go, bowling along the AutoRoute through France. We've already had the first argument – daughters and I do not want to use the French motor-way toilets. We can smell them from half a mile away and daughters are adamant – they refuse point blank to go anywhere near them and husband has to give in and let them use the toilet in the 'van – the one he tells us frequently *he* has to empty. Yes, and he can go on emptying it – that's definitely men's work and I'm not giving in on this one! He's got a point though – it's not pleasant – so I, for the sake of *Entente Cordiale,* agree to use the facilities (such as they are) on the AutoRoute. I realised long ago why French men can always be seen weeing by the side of the road. They don't have a strong enough nose to enter French latrines. But we British are made of sterner stuff and don't have continental habits.

Talk about cheating husbands – he heads off behind the lavatories to join other British men standing in a row in front of some bushes. So, I'm the only one brave enough to venture inside. To start with there's only half a door to cover your middle bits while performing. And two little foot places beside an evil smelling hole. This is where it gets difficult. You have to hold up the bottom of your trousers to keep them out of the wet and, at the same time, hold down the top of them while balancing on the foot-rests. All this while holding your breath, trying not to breathe, and clutching a hanky over your nose. Then – it's time to flush! This the French have got down to a fine art – it's automatic. There I am, choking and about to escape with trousers still clutched around my knees, when the automatic flush sends out a tidal wave on the scale of a tsunami, leaving me standing there ankle deep in whatever fluid they flush their toilets with. The wave of water gushes out under the door (now I know why there's a gap) taking me and my water-logged sandals with it. I really haven't got the hang of French toilets.

Finally, somehow, we make Germany. Gitzen-berg-weiler-hof Something – sounds nice and we make our way there. And it is – nice I mean. Very German. All the caravans have to line up with exact precision, not a tow bar out of alignment. All the awnings have to be spaced exactly as instructed and the cars parked alongside in a straight row. And it's clean – pristine! Toilets, showers, washing-up area, launderette, restaurant, swimming pool, all is immaculate. I'm well pleased!

Afternoon tea

But English customs will out. We can recognise the Brits in all the rows straightaway. Each day, around four o'clock, out come the tables and table-cloths and afternoon tea is enjoyed. Tables are set with tea-pots and china cups, and littles plates of biscuits and cakes. I'm sure if you could get sliced bread in Germany they'd have had little cucumber sandwiches – with the crusts cut off, of course – set out as well. We follow suit – can't let the side down – and it's lovely. At night we all sit outside our awnings enjoying a glass of wine (or a Babycham in my case) with little fairy lights flickering. Caravanning at its best.

Lake Constance is delightful with its garden island full of flowers. And we love the concerts held along the lake-side. Once again – all the chairs are lined up in precise rows, actually chained together so that nobody can disturb the pattern of them. Husband's perfect day out is our visit to Friedrichshafen Museum, birthplace of the Zeppelin airship, and we try to instil a history lesson into our daughters.

Daughters love it here. Each evening they have to help with the chores and their job is to take the washing-up over to the communal facilities where there is copious hot water and draining boards. This is helped, no doubt, by the fact that every child is similarly despatched to do this after the evening meal and they have a whale of a time together. Language presents no barrier when you're flicking sudsy water over each other! They take a long time washing-up!

But we do have our moments on that camp-site. Floods, following a monumental storm, inundate the site with unbelievable hostility. Tents, awnings, tables and chairs are tossed and swept away in a river of water running between the caravans. And so we say 'Goodbye' to Germany and head for Austria.

Austria – a land where there are outdoor swimming pools set in snow covered mountain villages. These are heated so that you can scoop up snowballs as you swim! Of bob-sleighs and cow bells, of gateau and leather *laden hose*.

And finally – Switzerland. First big mistake is that we stop for a drink and a cake. It costs the equivalent of £7 – it's the most expensive tea and cake we have ever had and their tea isn't up to much anyway. I feed the whole family for a week on that amount. Cost of living here is monumental!

And it's raining. The camp-site is a quagmire. We live in our wellies wading through mud. The site proprietor has organised duck-boards to put down in awnings so that we don't sink and be lost forever in the sludge. But there aren't enough to go round. As each pitch is vacated, all the men rush over and try and grab the duck-boards for their own use. We're British so totally miss out – we thought they would form a sort of queue and collect their allocation. We've a lot to learn here. I remember women in Germany elbowing us all out of the way in order to get on a train going up some mountain or other. We missed the train every time as we were permanently shoved to the back. Anyway, 'handbags at dawn' – we Brits have elbows too and eventually put them to good use. It's the same here – No "After you old chap" in this neck of the woods! Finally I keep watch for signs of people leaving and we come up with a strategy – we manage to get a few duck-boards for ourselves.

The sun eventually shines and all is good – even though we're on austerity rations because of the cost of food. The scenery is magnificent. Youngest daughter spends hours running behind the waterfall alongside the camp and eldest daughter is entranced by waking each morning and gazing up at the Jungfrau Mountain above us. Having the caravan has made all this possible.

But with Swiss Francs dangerously low, we must start to make our way back through Germany and France. First over-night stop in Germany is at a small site – very rural but clean with a miserable, bad-tempered, little hob-goblin in charge of it. We're dirty and tired after driving all day and we just want a shower and bed even though it's still daylight. So, first to the showers are Daughters Number One and Two. Now, the showers are little open-air wooden cubicles with a half door on the front for modesty sake. Heads and feet are clearly on view so that everybody knows when the shower is occupied. Having been gone sometime (I don't go looking for them because they can't come to any harm having a shower and I'm enjoying a Babycham in the sunshine), youngest daughter comes running across to us absolutely doubled up with laughter. Eldest daughter has got the door stuck in the shower and can't get out. The space under the door isn't quite big enough for her to get under and the space at the top is too small as well. Her clothes are in a heap somewhere outside and she can't quite reach them. We go back with youngest daughter, who is still creased up with laughter at the plight of her big sister, and push a towel and clothes under the door to save her any more embarrassment. We can't budge the door either. At this point we have to fetch the hob goblin. He is not amused – I'm glad we don't understand German. After a lot of heaving and grunting he

83

finally manages to lever the splintering wood door and it flies open. We leave the next morning.

But, just as much as husband likes going on holiday, I like coming home. And this is no exception. The dog is ecstatic to have us back even though she's been spoilt rotten by elderly relatives and the cat sulks because we've dared to go away. Why do we put ourselves through this each year?

But, if we're lucky, we all get to go on holiday. It's the opportunity for a family to spend quality time together, isn't it? Well, believe that and you'll believe anything. Marriages may be made in heaven but the seeds of divorce are definitely sown on holiday.

Please God let the holidays end soon so that I can go back to work.

HOME ECONOMICS

Now, I'm the first to admit that as a housewife I'm an abysmal failure. My Victoria sponge is mistaken for suet pudding, my baked potatoes have been known to break teeth, and my pathetic attempt at anything difficult like a Pavlova or gateau only provides a side-splitting episode of amusement for the entire family.

But if anything really saps my confidence it's the words 'Home Economics' eldest daughter bandies around. I remember 'Domestic Science', as it was called in the olden days when I went to school, simply conditioned girls to be 'good wives'!

At precisely 11.30 p.m., when I'm nicely asleep in front of the telly, she comes tripping down the stairs to present me with a list of ingredients she requires by 8.30 a.m. the following morning, and I spend a sleepless night with the realisation that the only item I can produce from the larder is the 'pinch of salt'. Dawn find me lurking on the neighbours' doorsteps with a begging bowl, grovelling for food.

"Oh, God, not again", moans long suffering husband to daughter, as she proudly presents us with an unset, undercooked, something or other in a biscuit tin. Last week though she actually made a perfect plate jam tart – well, it was perfect until another girl dropped a food mixer on top of it!

Perhaps if I had taken Domestic Science more seriously when I was at my under-performing secondary modern school I wouldn't be quite so inadequate now. I'm really good at sewing though. Our needlework teacher (nickname 'Sadistic Bitch') used to whack us with the cane if as much as one stitch was even ever so slightly out of line. You try sewing a fine seam with bleeding palms!

However, I do endeavour to put 'Home Economics' into action in our house. "Can you turn sheets 'sides to middle' yet", I ask. Apparently not (one mark to me). "Thank God for that", mutters husband, who has a permanent crease down his centre back as a result of laying on the half-inch thick French seam which joins my sheets 'sides to middle'.

"What about making face cloths out of old towels that have gone thin in the middle?" Another negative response. (Eldest daughter nil, me two).

"How about hammering 'Blakey's' into rubber heels to make them last longer … No?"

I'm feeling decidedly better already. In fact, a watery delusion of adequacy is definitely beginning to filter through. I know I'll never make 'housewife of the year', but perhaps my brand of home economics isn't quite such a failure after all!

NEVER ON A SUNDAY

Sunday – a day of rest – uh – that's a laugh for a start! Definitely male orientated.

What does Sunday conjure up for you? Thoughts of a lie-in, a perfumed bath, a stroll through hazy sunshine and dancing daffodils by a pretty village church, demure children in their Sunday best? Definitely a hat and high heels type of day.

Well, from the look of things, my cloud seven must have had an almighty wallop from a meteorite!

Husband is spending an idyllic morning flying his model 'plane. Daughters, still in bed, of course, have plugged some gadget into their ears which gives them a direct connection to the demented warblings of every pop group under the sun, instead of having to listen to me expounding on the joys of piano practice and the virtue of doing their homework.

And here I am, mid-Sunday morning, elegantly clad in my dressing-gown with the gravy stains, talking to myself, with the Hoover in one hand trying to suck up about half a ton of spilt sugar, and the hairdryer in the other, desperately endeavouring to defrost the chicken that I have forgotten to take out of the freezer.

Now, I quite like fish fingers with the Sunday roast potatoes, but my other half has this obsession about a roast joint for his lunch and for some reason objects to his Brussels sprouts floating in the tomato sauce from the tin of spaghetti hoops I have opened in desperation when all else has failed. And, if they all continue to glare at me and mutter when once again egg and chips replaces the cordon-bleu cuisine they are all expecting, I shall end up with a complex and a nervous twitch! That's the trouble with a family who live to eat when I only eat to live.

Perhaps I should get the hat and high heels out of moth-balls and totter along to church and spend a peaceful – if not quiet – half-hour composing the menu for the coming week.

And, please God, would you mind giving my cloud seven just a little nudge when it's time to dig the rissoles out of the freezer.

CHRISTMAS TREE CHIPOLATAS

I love tradition at Christmas, don't you? The magic of Father Christmas who manages to be in every high street, every school bazaar, and at every Christmas party, all at the same time, and who still has enough energy left to deliver all those presents on Christmas Eve!

The beautiful atmosphere created by children gathered round the crib singing 'Away in a Manger' to the traditional tune – I stand in silent protest at the new tunes aimed at 'with it' people – probably because I'm 'without it' (whatever 'it' is).

And, of course, chipolatas on the Christmas tree.

Now, you may be content with quite an ordinary tree, dancing with tinsel and fairy lights, with an angel on the top; but for the past thirty-odd years, which is as far back as I care to remember, our tree has danced with foil-wrapped cold sausages twinkling amongst the fairy lights! And, No ... it's not at all odd! I happen to come from a very 'doggy' family and although the dogs have changed over the years, all have received a present off the tree on Christmas Eve along with the rest of the family.

Every time the children select another chocolate novelty from the tree, the dog lines up for another sausage – nothing odd in that, to a doggy family, I assure you!

In view of the fact that girls usually carry on the family traditions when they marry, and the women of our family have produced nothing but daughters for the past five generations, I can see it won't be too long before chipolatas on the Christmas tree is a tradition that will spread across the nation.

And what about the presents. There I was the other night happily engrossed digging porridge out of the filter in the dishwasher, and half an eiderdown out of the filter in the washing-machine, when my other half asked what I wanted for Christmas.

Well, I know what I don't want! Last year he told all the elderly relatives that I wanted a dust-pan and brush set in a matching washing-up bowl. I got four — all wrapped in cellophane with a bow!

What about presents for the children? There they are, brain-washed every evening by watching the expensive electronic games advertised on the telly, and they are decidedly unimpressed by my story about the highlight of Christmas morning being an Enid Blyton book and an orange tucked in the toe of Grandad's sock!

Elderly relatives have been on the 'phone to ask what the Lord and Master wants for Christmas. "There are a few things he's been hankering after", I told them. "He'd be thrilled to bits with a new dustbin, an ironing board cover, or a pair of oven gloves".

My word, revenge is sweet! You should see his face on Christmas morning!

THE WILD WEST

"**A** dream holiday – that's what we'll have – a dream holiday – in America!" Has living in a totally female household finally and completely tipped him off his rocker? My first response is: "How can we afford it?" I don't actually know anybody who has gone to America for a holiday but I've heard that some do. Daughters can't believe what they're hearing – "Disneyland – we're going to Disneyland!"

And so the planning for this ambitious adventure begins. Husband has already been doing a bit of advance thinking. "We can ask your Mum and Dad and, if your sister would let her come, we could take your niece – the three girls get on well together". I'm surprised husband is thinking of including niece – he's never forgiven her for being sick in the back of his new car when she was two years old! But she's our gorgeous little 'Currant-Bun Face' – a nickname I gave her when she was just a toddler and her eyes would crinkle up with laughter, and we would love her to come. Although I'm working part-time now, money is still on the tight side but, with seven of us going, it will split the cost a bit. Eldest daughter, now twelve, and niece are the same age, and, along with youngest daughter, aged nearly nine, can't wait to ask their Granny and Grandad. And, it's decided, we're all off to America. The land of Elvis Presley and frothy-coffee!

Husband tracks down a Travel Agent to sort us out a Winnebago Camper-Van in America which will sleep seven. That takes some doing but finally it's arranged, we pay our deposit, and are assured it will be there waiting for us in San Francisco. I can't believe we're actually going to do this – fly all the way to America – who'd have thought our little family from the backwoods of England could do that. But it's 1980 and all things are possible.

The flight out is uneventful, apart from my mother using up the entire aircraft's allocation of sick-bags, and my Dad, who is asthmatic and unable to exert himself, means husband has to carry all seven suitcases. But, anyway, here we are, all seven of us, having survived unscathed and still together, the hostile American Customs Control, emerging through the airport doors into the San Francisco sunshine … and then the trouble starts!

There are cabs everywhere and instantly the drivers surround us. We are targeted because we look alien and lost and the drivers tout for business. Obviously two cabs will be needed and we try to ask each driver, all of whom are shouting in our ears, how much to drive us to the Holiday Inn. Next thing, we're surrounded by 'cops' all with hands hovering over holsters, because cab drivers aren't allowed to tout. Clearly they've picked on us because we don't know the rules of the game. Then the police question us for evidence of touting so that they can nick the drivers! All the other passengers from the flight have long disappeared and there we still stand, husband guarding seven suitcases, mother on the verge of throwing up again, Dad in imminent danger of a full-blown asthmatic attack, and me trying to shield daughters and niece from the hullabaloo.

Husband and girls are finally escorted to the first cab in the rank and roar off. Mum, Dad and me (along with the seven suitcases) are shoved into a second cab. It's at this stage I realise that husband has got the address of the hotel and there is more than one Holiday Inn in San Francisco. By some hair-raising miracle – not to mention 'jumping a red' – our maniac of a cab driver catches up with the one in front speeding along with the rest of the family sharing this white-knuckle ride through the back streets of San Francisco.

We drive through some really run-down graffiti-daubed neighbourhood and our driver tells us it's the 'gay' area and once we get to our hotel we should stay inside and not go out. Oh Great! We arrive; we don't want to risk going out as we've got into enough trouble as it is and we've only been here five minutes! It's getting dark anyway and the area looks decidedly dodgy – no, we won't venture out, especially with two old folk and three young girls. We'll have a meal in the hotel and then go to bed. Oh Yeah! Good thought. We're too late for the hotel restaurant and they won't even provide us with a sandwich – so much for American hospitality! I have one apple lurking in the bottom of my bag (don't know how that got through customs) and I divide it into seven sections and we say 'Goodnight' and go to bed hungry – Welcome to America!

Anyway, today's another day. We all have a nice, if somewhat strange, breakfast; pancakes with some sort of treacle poured over the top of a fried egg. All seems to be going to plan today. A big car arrives to take us to where the Winnebago Camper-Van is waiting for us. We all get in and we're on our way. Fine ... until we get to the middle of the Golden Gate Bridge and stop in traffic to see Alcatraz. That's scary. Being incarcerated in there must be some punishment! So, here we are, sitting in the traffic jam, getting a running commentary from the hippy driver, when the occupant of the car in front throws out a smouldering cigarette end. Our driver, full of righteous indignation and a death wish, leaps out of the car, leaving us stranded, to remonstrate with the driver in front. Oh God – here come the 'cops' again! Does everybody in America spend their lives waving their arms and yelling at each other! Thank goodness the traffic starts moving at this point or I'm sure we would all have ended up in Alcatraz.

Now, let's put our colourful start behind us – here, gleaming in the sun-shine in front of us, is this huge vehicle; 30 feet long, 8 feet wide, Winnebago. I've never seen anything like it. It's so modern. It has air-conditioning – imagine that – soft comfy bed-settees, a cooker, a fridge and a freezer so big you could house a polar bear in it. Sure beats the little ice-cream size freezer compartment at the top of my fridge at home. It's got a walk-in shower – wow – is this how all Americans live?

The Winnebago

The handover of the vehicle seems a bit casual, but I guess that's just the laid-back attitude endemic in America, and off we go. First step Hearst Castle – well, not quite! Fifty miles down the Pacific Highway and trouble hits. "Can you smell

94

gas?" Husband swerves into a service station where we hope to find a 'phone, and we evacuate the camper-van. With no gas-masks (that war-time relic still lurks in the cupboard back home) we take ourselves off to a safe distance the other side of the car-park and wait for the mechanic the Travel Company has arranged to come and fix it. After hours of hanging around we're off again. It's only when we try to settle for the night we find the supplier of the 'van has omitted to include any bedding – not a blanket or a pillow between us.

But we're British and, following in the steps of Columbus (who was actually Italian – but never mind) we proceed along The Pacific Highway. And very beautiful it is. Monterey, Santa Barbara, Hearst Castle – it's all on our list. Away from the city everybody is really friendly – they "Just love your accent" and ask what part of Australia we're from … Australia? I don't think Americans are very worldly. And finally – the fulfilment of a dream – I get to sit on Malibu Beach in my new bikini!

And now, the culmination of the children's dreams – Disneyland. We pull into the allocated area for camper-vans – lovely – so well organized and then … 'Cops' waving guns everywhere racing around the car-park chasing some felon who they finally corner and spread-eagle across the bonnet of a car – I make the children lay on the floor of the 'van imagining bullets pinging through the windscreen at any moment. The car-park resembles a gun-fight at the OK Corral without Wyatt Earp in charge.

But finally law and order is established and we leave the relative safety of the camper-van and are first in the queue

95

for Disneyland. And it's wonderful. We all love every moment of it. 'The Submarine Voyage', 'The Chair-Lift Through The Matterhorn', 'Hyperspace Mountain' and all the larger than life Disney characters – it's endless spectacle – pure magic. My mother, who was apprehensive and thought there would be nothing there to interest her and Dad, was the biggest 'kid' of all. Midnight saw her running up Disney's Main Street trying to cram in another go on the 'Haunted Mansion' before it closed. The 'Electric Parade' – I can't describe it – we have nothing to compare back home, and the fireworks over 'Sleeping Beauty's Castle' are images that I hope the children will retain for ever. I know I shall – it's been the most exciting day in all our lives. Dreamland at Margate will never seem the same again!

Disneyland

Now it's inland and we're crossing the Nevada Desert on the way to Las Vegas – and disaster strikes. It's 112 degrees Fahrenheit and that's hot! Here we are, bowling along the freeway, when – bang – the cap flies off the radiator and is lost forever, along with all the water from the engine's cooling system, and the camper-van shudders to a halt. What do we do in the middle of a desert? Husband, undaunted and daft as a brush, says he remembers seeing a filling station a couple of miles back and he could walk there and get a screw top for the radiator. We have a domestic water supply so we could use that to fill up again.

He gets out of the 'van and starts to walk back in the direction from which we have come. The heat is dazzling and as his image fades in the distance it starts to shimmer and blur. My mother is convinced he's succumbed to the heat and collapsed and I start trying to flag down passing motorists to get help. Finally a car stops and this lovely couple offer to back their car along the hard-shoulder to find husband. He's not fallen over – in fact he is found in the service station buying the screw top. Our rescuers are very kind but they obviously think we're three ha'pence short of a shilling because there, on a big sign, it says, *'If you break down, stay in your vehicle and await rescue'*. They patiently explain to us that freeways across the desert are patrolled by helicopter as it is unsafe to get out of the car. The big sign also says in large letters *'This is rattle-snake country'*. Oh to be in England – it's much more civilised than America. Only bunny-rabbits hop across our roads.

And on we go to Las Vegas. My Dad, who didn't realise that heat like this is possible, has stopped off at a Thrift Store (Charity Shop in our language) and bought an outsize pair of shorts and is now walking around looking like Mr. Magoo. The girls are in fits! He's also having trouble understanding the freezer. I've lost count of the number of times he's asked where the ice-cubes are kept! At least the heat seems to agree with his asthma and Mother's stopped being travel sick!

Finally – Las Vegas. We do 'The Strip' in a bus where Mum sits in terrified silence as the elderly man sitting next to her has a gun. What's the matter with these people? Imagine pensioners carrying guns on a Number 11 bus going up the high street in England. But I can't wait to get out of Las Vegas – I'm certainly not passing over any of my hard earned dollars in some gambling den of iniquity! The shows look spectacular though – the lights dazzling and the noise deafening – but it's brash and hot!

So, off we go again via The Hoover Dam which is huge and on to The Grand Canyon which is incredible. The Colorado River weaving its way like a ribbon at the bottom of the Canyon, the sheer scale of it all is amazing. You can get vertigo just looking down on it. I've got this amazing new Polaroid camera – it takes up to twelve photos and the print comes out of the bottom of it in an instant and I've been saving it to take pictures of The Grand Canyon.

Finally, we're heading back to San Francisco, intending to take in Yosemite National Park en route. This is where big trouble is brewing. First of all we upset quite a lot of tourists going up the hill as we didn't know it's a rule of the highway to pull over if you have more than a few cars behind you and let them pass. Our camper-van doesn't go very fast and we build up quite a long queue of angry motorists tailing us. American ladies (especially large ones) can be quite vitriolic – husband's ears are still burning. We find a nice camping spot and I reserve our emplacement by putting a yellow table-cloth with red cherries on it on the wooden table-bench allocated to each pitch.

And then niece announces she has a sore throat and tummy-ache. As this appears to be getting worse we leave our table-cloth to reserve our pitch and all drive down to the Medical Centre. Back home we'd be prescribed a hot-water-bottle and a couple of aspirin – not America – they make a big event out of everything. Next thing we know is that an ambulance has been summoned and niece, with me hanging on to her, is bundled on a stretcher in the back of it with an accompanying nurse. I guess the doctors can see the medical insurance dollars accumulating before their very eyes.

This has got to be the scariest moment of our lives. I have no money on me, only the clothes I stand up in, and I haven't a clue where they're taking us. Now I recognise that ambulances in England flash blue lights and clang bells, but this is ridiculous – all for a tummy-ache and a sore throat. We have to go along with this drama because they are talking about the possibility of an appendicitis and, of course, that could be serious – but Americans are so trigger-happy and they panic!

The nice nurse tells me that we are going to a hospital some forty miles away. How will husband know where we are – do I have authority to sign forms for my lovely little niece to have parts of her removed? The journey in the ambulance is traumatic – even those with nerves of steel would have them shattered by this frenetic journey. In England people get out of the way for an ambulance – not in America. The driver is constantly clanging bells, wailing his siren and flashing all his lights – blue or otherwise – at motorists who refuse to get out of his way. He is also in touch, via his radio, with local police and keeps up a running report of the number-plates of the cars who do not move to let him through so that they can, presumably, apprehend them for impeding the progress of an ambulance. Oh God, not more 'cops' running around waving guns!

But in all of this, niece, who has forgotten to be ill for a moment, and I, are riveted by the report from the police coming through on the ambulance radio. Apparently there's this poor 'guy' holed up in his apartment with a rattle-snake threatening to strike him down. Police are surrounding the building — another stand-off at the OK Corral! We hear that they shoot the rattle-snake and rescue the gibbering idiot who has been incarcerated in the apartment. I think I'd be more frightened of the 'cops'!

We finally make the hospital. The poor nurse will be making the return trip back to Yosemite — she seems to take all this in her stride. I plead with her to locate husband and tell him where we are or we'll never meet up again. Niece is wheeled into a corridor — and it's awful. I don't know what type of down-town hospital this is but it's certainly not one with carpet on the floor. Perhaps they don't think the insurance will pay up. The passage way is filled with drunks, addicts and other dregs of humanity, all yelling and screaming. It's pandemonium. There is vomit on the floor. I'm supposed to go back to Yosemite with the nurse but how can I leave my niece here among this lot. No ... I wouldn't leave my own children here and I'm certainly not leaving my sister's child in these circumstances — so I stand guard and glare at anybody who ventures near us.

Having established that niece has tonsillitis, we're eventually taken to a ward. It's a four bedded room — I think the three other occupants are Mexican — they don't speak to us. An attendant in a none-too-clean white suit tries to persuade me to leave but I'm not going anywhere – I've no money, no transport, not the foggiest idea where I am – so – where am I supposed to go anyway! Finally the attendant produces a canvas camp bed and I'm allowed to bunk down next to niece who has become strangely quiet (not like her) all of a sudden. What this hospital needs is an English dragon of a matron in a pristine apron and a starched cap, who can put the fear of God into anybody not performing to her rigid standards. This is the other side of America!

Next morning, I almost cry with relief when husband walks in the door – I really thought I'd never see him again and have to remain destitute in America for the rest of my life. That kind nurse did seek him out and tell him where we had been taken. Thank you God! And niece, better or not – we're out of here ... NOW!

It's only two days before our flight home and we've a long way to go. Only our yellow table-cloth with the red cherries gets to enjoy a stay in Yosemite!

You can keep the bright lights of Las Vegas – I'm going back to Bognor next year.

RESOLUTIONS

Don't know what happened to the resolutions I made in 1980 about not shrieking at the daughters, being nice at least some of the time to my other half, and emptying the Hoover bag before it bursts and empties its contents all over me. Perhaps I'm not a very resolute person, but here I go again for 1981:

1. I will try to stop ruining the family's viewing of Dallas by making facetious remarks about Pamela and Sue-Ellen (nickname 'Swellin') even though they make me sick. They're just not like real people. Coronation Street is more my level.

2. I will try not to put elderly relatives through the car windscreen when I jam on the brakes to avoid a geriatric rabbit doing a kamikaze hop across the Reading Road. (That's going to be a non-starter – how could I run over a bunny-rabbit? Elderly relatives always bounce back in their seats anyway).

3. I will not waste energy threatening the daughters when I can't find their bed-room floor to Hoover. If they want an obstacle race in order to get into bed – that's up to them. They'll never make good house-wives at this rate! Perhaps it's my fault – I obviously haven't set them a good example.

4. I will iron every part of my husband's shirt instead of just the front, so that he can take his jacket off sometimes when he gets hot instead of risking heat exhaustion. I tried to get eldest daughter to iron his shirts once – he

ended up with half a dozen tram-lines down his sleeves. No, it's probably best he keeps his jacket on.

5. I will try not to glare at people who smoke all over me (I hate smoking) and I will choke quietly so as to cause them as little discomfort as possible. But why are smokers' rights more important than my wanting to breathe fresh-air? I know smoking is supposed to keep your weight down and is good for the nerves, but second-hand smoke doesn't do my nerves any good!

6. I will try to resist the temptation to empty all my loose change into every collection tin for every charitable cause for miles around so that it's a wonder, by the end of the week, me and mine aren't dining out at the nearest Salvation Army's soup kitchen for the destitute. But collectors shake their cans and smile so nicely at me that it's difficult to look the other way.

7. I will 'doggedly' continue to cling to the euphoric belief that everybody loves my dog as much as I do. It's members of the human race who pollute the air, the ocean, and kick beer cans up the high street, and do far more to devastate the environment than she can with an occasional biodegradable little mistake.

8. I will smile nicely at the mostly male drivers who race up behind me and sit on my tail at ninety miles an hour along the Binfield Road and make rude signs at me just because my brake lights flash on and off trying to avoid the sparrows having their breakfast. (I'm not running sparrows over either!)

9. I will not lower the tone of the neighbourhood by shrieking like a fish-wife at those who light bonfires over me. I accept that I'm just a lazy person wanting to sunbathe and have tea in the garden on a rare, warm, sunny Sunday afternoon. (They light bonfires on Mondays too when I've got the washing out!)

10. Final resolution (made for me by husband) – I will learn to love the three million bits of model aeroplane he has been in the middle of making for the last twenty years; and when he manages to fly the things, will contentedly spend frozen hours tramping round the country-side looking for those he has lost. (He doesn't think much of my suggestion to fly them inside big plastic bags so that all the bits stay together when he crashes them).

Well, that's my resolutions for 1981 settled. All I need do now is write out a list for the rest of the family. Only one thing stops me – they never keep them!

FROM ROOTS TO WINGS

Reflecting back on family life through the 70's nearly fifty years on, with all the ups and downs, good times, funny times, sad times; through childhood illnesses, when eldest daughter's temperature soars to 106 degrees and we're distraught with worry, when youngest swallows a boiled sweet and chokes and I thank God I know the Heimlich Manoeuvre and probably save her life; through measles, mumps and knocks and bumps, I'm amazed they survive. But they do in spite of us, and they now pass on the values they learnt to their own children.

There's no blue-print for family life, it's a bumbling muddle of trial and error. Babies don't arrive with an instruction manual stapled to their umbilical. With the benefit of hindsight, I expect we could have done better, but we've done our best. I hope our children don't judge us too harshly when deciding which care home to put us in!

We have the overwhelming responsibility to teach them right from wrong, to treat others as they would like to be treated, to guide them through childhood days and teenage years and provide them with a secure and happy home in which to flourish. The best we can do is give our children firm roots and encourage them to grow wings and fly.

The most precious gift we can give a child is the gift of love and that we give unconditionally and by the bucket load.

I hope you've enjoyed stumbling through the seventies with me.